MW00440250

Christmas in Sweetwater County – Sweetwater County Series
Ciara Knight
ISBN-13: 978-1-939081-15-5

Christmas in Sweetwater County

Book V
Sweetwater County
Series

Ciara Knight

Also by Ciara Knight

The Neumarian Chronicles
Weighted
Escapement
Pendulum
Balance

Battle For Souls
Rise From Darkness
Fall From Grace
Ascension of Evil

www.ciaraknight.com

ACKNOWLEDGMENTS

This novel would not be possible without the endless dedication of so many. A special thank you to: Karen Wake, a valued street team member and special guest in this story, my family, friends and my special street team members Colleen Everly, Maranda Raven Melton, Ariyanna Moon, Rosemary Hendry, Tara Pennington, Sarah Moore and Amanda Price.

CHAPTER ONE

The huge Christmas star at the top of the Creekside Courthouse clock tower not only illuminated the darkening sky, but warmed Cathy Mitchell's heart. She sighed in relief then settled back against the leather driver's seat and read the welcome sign to Sweetwater County aloud as she always did when returning home. *"Welcome to Sweetwater County, Tennessee. Where your heart and home belong."*

She had never appreciated the town motto more than she did at that moment. Who knew only driving a few hours away from home would lead to such a world of mess? From now on, there would be no more driving out of town, no more internet, and most of all, no more dating sites. She had more than learned her lesson.

What was I thinking to let Rose talk me into this?

Her phone played the chorus of *My Boyfriend's Back*—her best friend, Judy Benjamin's ringtone—but she ignored it. Judy could wait a few more minutes to laugh at Cathy's poor judgment. Besides, she wasn't ready to talk about her date with the overly forward man who didn't look anything like his picture. Of course, she didn't exactly weigh a hundred and twenty-five pounds like her profile said, but a lady's weight was between her and the scale.

The road grew dark with the setting sun, the gray clouds overhead were just beginning to dump their load. She flicked on the windshield wipers, but the cold evening air quickly fogged up the car's windows, making it difficult to see. She eyed the unfamiliar console. *Oh, how I miss my Caddy*, she thought, trying to keep one eye on the road while she searched for the defogger button.

She still grieved its demise, despite the fact it was sacrificed for a good cause. She'd rammed her precious cream-colored Cadillac into that scumbag's car when he'd tried to kidnap Trianna Shaw, Sheriff Mason's fiancé. Cathy didn't regret her decision, but even so, she missed it. If only the insurance had paid more. Who knew that five minutes after you drove a new car off the lot it lost thirty percent of its value. And with her current financial situation, there was no way she could afford to buy a new one.

She spotted a button with an illuminated triangle and pressed it, but instead of the fog clearing, orange light flashed on and off over the dark two-lane road. It looked ominous, reminding her of a thrasher movie Judy made her watch one night when her husband, James, was out of town. They ended up staying awake all night, and she had never been able to look at the Benjamin farm the same way again. The once tranquil piece of land now harbored the worst spooks her imagination could conjure.

With her heartbeat quickening, she turned off the

hazards and eyed the dashboard again. After careful analysis, she decided the button next to the heater must be the right one and pressed it. Instantly, heat blasted from the floorboards.

With a huff, she hit the button again then tried the one next to it and the white haze covering her windshield started to retreat. Leaning over to peer through the clear portion at the bottom, she saw a small rodent skitter across the road. She let out a yelp and swerved, her phone sliding across the seat onto the floor. "Lord have mercy!"

Her phone rang again, but she wasn't about to bend over to retrieve it while driving. Instead, she returned her hands to the ten and two position on the steering wheel and drove around the last winding curve into town.

White lights, tacked along the storefronts, sparkled along the street. She slowed to admire the Christmas tree hogging the display window at J & L Antiques. Large gold balls covered most of the greenery, while red and gold ribbon cascaded down the tree from the bright star at the top. Eyeing the rest of the storefronts, she had to give Judy credit. Her best friend really knew how to decorate for the holidays. Of course, she'd never admit it. Judy's head would swell larger than a pregnant cow.

A few stores further, she pulled into a parking spot in front of her favorite haunt, Café Bliss. On an evening like this, everyone in town would be sipping coffee or tea around the little bistro tables that filled the coffee shop. And if she knew Judy, which she did, she'd be sitting by the window, sipping her London Fog and staring at the mountains.

Despite the cold, rainy weather, crowds of people littered the sidewalks, no doubt shopping for Christmas gifts. A large, obtrusive *Grand Re-Opening* sign hung from the front of the newly re-constructed knitting store at the corner.

"Only gone for a few days and the town's already going to Hell in a hand basket," Cathy muttered to herself.

Several months after a series of tornadoes hit, the town finally looked put back together. Even though many still grieved at the loss of loved ones killed in the disaster last summer, at least they didn't have to look at the rubble left behind any longer. It was why she pushed so hard to return the town to its original glory— minus the obnoxious new signs. It was the least she could do to help her friends and neighbors heal.

With her purse slung over her shoulder and an umbrella in hand, Cathy opened the car door and stepped into a massive mud puddle. Good thing she was wearing boots, instead of her usual dress shoes. Judy had insisted on taking her shopping to get some updated clothes before her big day. Since she didn't want the entire town knowing she was broke, she went along for the ride, but still came home with more than she should have. At least the boots were a gift, an early Christmas present from Judy. Cathy had to admit, they did make her calves look smaller, and she felt younger, too.

Thankfully, the downpour had turned to a mild

drizzle, and she was able to make it inside the café without getting too wet. She'd never cared that much about being dressed up. Constantly fussing over what to wear and if this looked good with that, seemed like a big waste of time to Cathy. After all, what was wrong with kitten sweatshirts and tennis shoes? She preferred her long, loose skirts and comfy shoes to Judy's heels and power suits. But now, she also liked the world of leggings and boots. Who knew you could look fashionable and still be comfortable?

She smiled to herself and held her head a little higher than she had leaving Knoxville. Even if she wasn't perfectly dressed like Judy, or had a man that loved her with all his heart like Trianna and Lisa, she still had a good life in Sweetwater County with her friends.

As Cathy had suspected, the café was bustling. Trianna and Sheriff Mason were huddled in the corner, holding hands while looking over a wedding magazine, something Cathy thought she'd never see Jimmy Mason do after his first wife left him. But from the moment Cathy spotted Trianna, she knew the girl was perfect for him. Of course, if Cathy hadn't meddled, Trianna would have left town and Sheriff Mason would still be a confirmed bachelor.

"Hey, Cathy," Trianna chimed.

Cathy forced a smile and waved, but couldn't help noticing Trianna hadn't gotten rid of that ridiculous purple streak in the front of her hair. She sighed inwardly. *I sacrificed my car to save her life. You'd think the woman would take my fashion advice.* There was no reason for her to still have it. Trianna had already taken down the Atlanta company that had murdered her brother and there were no more assassins left in their sleepy little town.

Cathy made a mental note to book a hair appointment for Trianna prior to the wedding. She couldn't let the poor girl get married looking like that.

She scanned the shop, spotting the owner, Mrs. Fletcher, and Becca, her newest barista, but there was no sign of Lisa, Eric, James, or Judy. Strange. She was sure that Judy at least would be here.

The aroma of peppermint invited her further into the coffee house. Cathy placed her damp umbrella in the bucket next to the door and made her way through the crowd to the front counter. As she passed, she nodded at Karen Wanke, the church secretary, sitting at a table with Connie, Eric Gaylord's secretary. *Oh gosh, I hope the dampness in the air doesn't cause my hair to spiral out of control like Connie's.*

"Wow, it's hopping in here this evening," Cathy said to Mrs. Fletcher, who nodded and set to work concocting some drink with steamed milk.

The new girl, Becca, stood at the register. "Can I help you, ma'am?"

Cathy chuckled. "You can just call me *Cathy*, Becca."

"Ms. Cathy, then. What can I get for you?" Becca scribbled the word *Cathy* onto a cup and Cathy sighed again.

As if Mrs. Fletcher doesn't already know my name. "I'll do one of those peppermint Mocha choca thingies."

"A Peppermint Mocha? What size?"

"Medium," Cathy answered, while eyeing the letters tattooed on Becca's fingers. *L-O-V-E. I'm all for love*, she thought, *but why does the girl need it written on her hand?*

"Do you want whip cream?"

Cathy nodded.

"One Grande Pep Mocha for Cathy," she yelled and set the cup next to the espresso machine.

"That must've hurt." Cathy pointed to Becca's fingers. "I mean, there's no meat on your fingers. Heck, there's no meat on any of you. I get a shot in my fat derrière and I want to cry. You must be one brave girl."

Becca laughed, a sweet, quiet kind of laugh, so unexpected from a troubled teen who sought refuge in a small town. "I don't know about being brave. My father called it stupid. I won't admit it to him, but I think he was right."

"Well, you seem to be doing well now, darling. You settling into Sweetwater? I heard you started taking some classes at the junior college over in Riverbend."

"Yes, ma'am. I mean, Ms. Cathy." She smiled. "I hope to learn a lot while I'm here."

Becca's cheerful tone sounded forced, making Cathy pause and study her expression. *Is the girl up to something?* The way her lips pressed together and her eyes darted to the floor then to the door made Cathy think the girl was going to cause some sort of trouble. Becca had abnormally large eyes, the kind you saw in those fashion magazines, so maybe that was why she looked nervous all the time.

"You didn't bring trouble into our town now, did you?" Cathy asked, trying to sound teasing.

Becca shook her head and met Cathy's gaze with a steady, practiced expression. "No. Of course not."

"Well, if you ever need anything," Cathy offered.

Just then, the bell above the door rang and a swift breeze caught the back of Cathy's legs. She turned to see a man around her age, with dashing peppered hair and dark eyes, standing at the door. His gaze traveled the room, eventually settling on Cathy. With a steady gate, he walked straight to her with purpose. He stood a good six inches taller than her. His face, although lined with age, was breathtaking, a Cary Grant or John Wayne kind of handsome.

"Hello," he said in a deep sensual voice.

"H-hi." Cathy smoothed her scarf, taking a moment to collect herself. Had this man spotted her from outside and come in to talk to her? Heck, her late husband, God rest his soul, would've never even noticed she was there. He'd passed by her many times throughout their thirty years of marriage without noticing.

"I'm sorry to trouble you, but wasn't there a young woman working behind the register just now?"

Cathy felt her elation deflate. What kind of lunacy had gotten into her? Why would he be coming to see her? Perhaps it was the aftereffects from her recent fiasco in dating. Complete with public humiliation, a shattered ego, and a bruise on her hip.

She shook her head to free it of the embarrassing

memories and turned to the counter. "Yes, she's right..." Mrs. Fletcher stood at the register, Becca nowhere to be seen.

"Can I help you with something, sir?" Mrs. Fletcher wiped her hands on her apron.

"He was looking for—"

"Yes. A coffee, please. Black." The man pulled a leather wallet from the back pocket of his pressed, grey pants and handed her a twenty. "It's busy in here."

Mrs. Fletcher took the money and opened the register. "Yep, December is always the busiest time of the year, especially on shopping days."

"Looks like the entire town is here." He gestured to the tables full of patrons.

Cathy saw Becca poke her head out the back office door then appeared again before the man turned around.

"Are you looking for someone in particular?" Cathy asked.

"Here's your change, sir." Mrs. Fletcher held out the man's money while shooting her a warning glance.

What's going on around here?

Cathy touched his arm as he reached to take his change. "I know everyone in town if you need help with something."

The man tensed, but then offered her a crooked, James Dean kind of smile, the kind that welcomed you closer, yet warned of danger.

Despite his reaction, she didn't remove her hand. There was something going on, and if Becca was in any trouble, Cathy was determined to help her.

White steam billowed up from the espresso machine. "I'll have that for you at the end," Mrs. Fletcher called out.

"No, not really," the man said, turning to Cathy. "I'm just scouting out the town since there is a potential job opportunity nearby." He took her hand and placed it in the crook of his arm then escorted her to the end of the counter.

Cathy's heart did a happy dance. The man was suave and definitely knew how to treat a woman. "Where would you be working?"

Before he could answer, Mrs. Fletcher appeared with coffee cups in hand. "Here you go."

With that, he let her go and handed her a cup then took the other for himself. "As a dean of the humanities department at the community college in Riverbend."

"Oh, how exciting."

The man took a sip of his coffee then licked his lips. "Well, this is unexpected."

Cathy giggled. "Oh well, I'd be happy to answer any questions you have about the town."

"The coffee...it's peppermint." He smiled and handed her his cup to exchange them.

Heat flooded Cathy's cheeks. "Well, I wish you all the luck." To hide her embarrassment, she quickly opened her handbag to pretend to look for something and noticed her phone blinking with a message. "That reminds me, I need to return Judy's call."

"Well, I won't keep you then." His eyes captivated her, and the way he looked down at her made her feel like the only person in the shop. "And thanks for the

10

offer. I'll be sure to find you, uh, Miss..."

"Cathy. Cathy Mitchell." She offered her hand and they shook, his grip strong and warm, yet gentle.

"Cathy," he nodded. "I'm Devon West. It's been a pleasure. I'll let you return that phone call now." He sauntered off with a Humphrey Bogart kind of air and sat at a table near Trianna and Jimmy.

When she finally cleared the fog enough to lift her phone, she noticed five missed calls. She looked at Mrs. Fletcher. "Geesh, can't she wait five more minutes to tease me about my God awful date with Mr. Handsy?" She stole a quick glance at Mr. Devon West and chuckled. "Perhaps I'll have better news soon."

Mrs. Fletcher's eyes shot wide then she bit her bottom lip, as if unsure of what to say.

Cathy knew that look well. *Can't decide whether to spill or not, huh? Nothing a little prodding won't fix.*

She'd just opened her mouth to ask when her phone rang. "It's Judy again," she mumbled to herself.

Mrs. Fletcher cleared her throat. "I think you better get that."

Cathy sighed then hit the *talk* button. "Hi, girl. What's going on?"

Silence.

"Judy?"

"It's Amelia," Judy croaked, a deep sadness plaguing her voice.

A sting of fear shot through Cathy and she froze. She hadn't heard that tone in her best friend's voice since the day Judy received word that the love of her life was missing in action and presumed dead during the Vietnam War.

"What's wrong?" If anything had happened to that little baby...

"I don't want to tell you over the phone. Where are you?" Judy asked.

Cathy eyed Mrs. Fletcher who kept her attention on the man near the window. "I'm at Café Bliss."

"Stay put. I'll be right there."

She hung up then carried her cup to the only table that remained free. Cathy took a sip of her peppermint mocha then realized she wasn't the first to drink from the cup. A shiver of something long dead inside her drew her attention back to the strange man only a few tables away.

CHAPTER TWO

Devon sipped his coffee, trying not to stare at the front counter, but he could have sworn his daughter was there only moments ago. After all these months, could he really have tracked her down? The young woman he'd seen through the café's front window was thin and tall like his daughter, and even possessed the same graceful movement.

How he missed the days of watching her perform. His mind slipped back to images of her dancing on stage, with her pink ballet shoes and little pink tutu, her long blond hair pulled up into a bun.

If only she'd let him speak to her.

"You okay?"

Devon's head shot up and he found the woman he'd been speaking to at the counter. Okay, he'd been interrogating her for information, but that was beside the point. The tight leggings and knee-high boots looked good on her. Most women around his age wore granny clothes and had no personality left, as if they'd been dried up. "I'm fine."

The woman ran a finger along her ear to tuck a blonde strand back into place. "I didn't mean to bother you, but can I ask you a question?"

He stood and pulled the chair out for her. "Please. Have a seat."

She smiled with such a glow about her, as if she could take on the world. "Okay, I only have a few minutes, though."

"Then they'll be the best few minutes of my day." He was rewarded with another smile, a slight blush tinting her cheeks.

"How come you're hanging around here? I mean, you don't seem like the type to be looking for a job in backwoods Tennessee."

He couldn't help but roar with laughter. If the woman only knew how true that statement was. He would have avoided this place entirely if he could have. Growing up in Connecticut, he had no desire to live in the south. He'd always believed the people there were hillbillies who still thought the civil war was being fought. Yet, once again, his daughter had challenged him to be a better man, to keep an open mind and accept things that were different.

"Let's just say I need a change."

"Midlife crisis?" Cathy asked. She sat tall in her seat and looked him directly in the eyes. He respected a woman that could maintain eye contact and not shy away. At the university, it was mostly men in his department. There was always the occasional student that had a crush on him, but they were way too young and lacked life experiences. He'd learned that lesson the hard way.

"Hardly," he chuckled. "Is this an inquisition?"

Cathy crossed her arms over her chest. "Yes."

An inner spark of admiration glimmered at the woman's tenacity. She had spunk and fire. He could respect that. "Are you always so direct?"

"You have no idea," she muttered. "Now, back to why you're here." Cathy sat forward and tapped her finger to the lid of her coffee. "You're looking for someone, I can guess that much. A lost...love interest?" Cathy's lip curled in the corner slightly, as though she was disgusted by her own question.

Devon shifted in his seat, not something he ever did when being questioned. Usually, he didn't care what people thought. Yet, he had this desire to set the woman straight. "So, you think I'm some sort of pedophile."

Cathy's face filled with surprise, which seemed feigned to him. "Sir, I accused you of no such thing."

He sat forward, leaning his elbow on the tabletop. "Then what are you implying, Ms. Mitchell?"

She wavered, the way most women did when he moved in close, but she quickly sat up straight again, adjusting her royal blue scarf, a color that made her eyes pop. "I'm not implying anything, Mr. West. I'm telling you that I've got your number. You might be good looking, and debonair, but that charm and knee-weakening smile will only take you so far. If you're here to make any sort of trouble, you best skedaddle out of my town."

This woman was something else. He found himself leaning back, away from her analyzing gaze. He studied her light hair and bright eyes and couldn't help but glance at her left hand, a habit he'd picked-up after his wife ran out on him six years ago. He liked flings, but he didn't like trouble. "What kind of trouble do you imagine me bringing here?"

"I don't imagine anything, Mr. West. You waltzed in here, asking about a young woman in my town, with no explanation. I want to know why."

Devon opened his mouth to confess, but then snapped it shut. *What am I doing?* He had already tried to get others to help bring his daughter home, but they'd all eventually given up. No, he had to do this on his own. His daughter needed help, and he wouldn't give up on her. After all, she was all he had left. He couldn't lose her, too.

He took a sip of his coffee then leaned over the table and, with the smoothness he'd perfected over the last few years, said, "I thought I saw someone I knew back home. But as you and the lady behind the counter stated, it was my mistake. Unless you lied for some reason."

She huffed. "That ain't gonna work on me. I call BS. You better start talking, or I'll make sure you're run out of town for good. You might be great eye-candy, but that don't mean I'll tolerate you stirring up trouble. We've had enough of that lately."

"I didn't realize you were the mayor here."

Cathy smiled then, mimicking his cool tone, said, "I'm much worse than any politician. I don't have the confines of public image or the law to keep me from killing you and burying you off some trail in the woods. You make the mistake of messing with my town, and I can assure you of one thing."

He quirked an eyebrow. "What's that?"

"I can and will have you removed from this town. The only question is whether it will be in a body bag." Cathy's face instantly morphed from serious and warning to soft and welcoming. "Well, I'm glad we've had this little chat. It's been a pleasure getting to know the man behind that playboy smile."

Playboy?

She said it with such venom in her voice, too, but he didn't care. What did it matter what this woman thought of him? Yet, for some reason, he opened his mouth to argue the point then thought better of it. None of this mattered unless she'd help him get his daughter back.

Cathy gathered her purse and coffee then started to rise, but Devon clasped her hand to keep her seated. "You mean my knee-weakening smile?"

A cold breeze swept through the coffee shop. He was sure it came from the front door opening, but the freezing gaze Cathy Mitchell gave him made him think otherwise.

"Don't play games with me, Mister. You might think I'm some sort of desperate widow that will fall at your feet in worship, but you've got another thing coming. I'm not that girl."

"Making friends again, I see." A petite woman with auburn hair appeared beside their table.

Cathy pulled her hand away and stood. "Mr. West and I were just having a little chat, is all. I was officially welcoming him to our town. I wanted to make sure he knew that I'd be the one to speak to if he ever needed anything."

The woman offered her hand. "It's a pleasure. I'm Judy Benjamin."

"You must be the phone call." He stood and took her hand. It was delicate and sweet, but lacked the fire he saw in Cathy.

"Huh? Oh, yes. And it only took seven tries to get her to call me back." Judy smirked at Cathy.

He released her hand, noticing Cathy's left eye twitching. Her hand reached up to Judy's arm in a consolatory gesture. "Well, ladies. I won't keep you."

A line had formed in front of the counter. The woman he assumed was the manager or owner tended to the register and drink orders all on her own. With this crowd, he knew that wasn't going to cut it. For the woman's sake, he decided it was better to leave and allow the woman in the back office, he was sure was his daughter, to return to work. Now wasn't the time for an intervention. There were too many people around, and the woman behind the counter obviously wanted to protect Becca from him. But why? What did Becca say to make her cover for her?

He turned toward the door, stepping over a cluster of brightly colored Christmas bags. Then a hand grasped his upper arm, stopping him.

"Wait."

His pulse rose at her touch. Probably because he hoped she'd help him with his daughter.

"You remember what I said." Cathy squeezed his arm tighter.

The woman had spunk, and God help him, he liked it. This was a woman that would be challenging, and he loved a challenge. He bent over and took her hand, pressing a kiss to her knuckles. "I think I'll need you to come around and remind me."

Judy shuffled away, suppressing a giggle.

Cathy smiled for a second then straightened. "Nice try, but my knees aren't even the tiniest bit wobbly." She tugged her hand free, took her coffee from the table, and sashayed over to where Judy sat.

Interest in the sassy woman across the room mocked his resolve, but he couldn't afford any distractions. He needed to focus on his daughter, not some bright blue-eyed gem in the coalmine of his existence.

Disregarding the light drizzle, he walked across the street and stood behind an old-fashioned street lamp. The charm of the town wasn't lost on him. The two-story brick storefronts were adorned with Christmas lights and cedar garlands and he could hear Bing Crosby crooning from somewhere down the street. It was like something out of one of those old movies he used to love to watch with Becca.

How did things go so wrong between them? They'd been so close.

He waited in the dark shadow cast by the street lamp and watched through the café's front window. Not only was he worried about scaring off Becca, but he didn't want to be exposed to Cathy's wrath either. He had no doubt she'd stomp from the coffee shop, take him by the ear and march him straight out of town if she saw him loitering. But a part of him kind of hoped she would.

He sighed at his timing. Finally, he'd met a woman that challenged him, but he had to meet her while on a mission to save his daughter.

Then he spotted the young woman he'd seen earlier behind the counter again. She had bleached her hair and looked thinner than he remembered, but that was his little girl. He longed to take her in his arms, but it wouldn't do any good. Something brought her to this town and he needed to know what it was so he could help her get through her grief and move on with life.

If only his wife had been stronger, but she hadn't and now Becca searched for something to fill the void her mother had left behind. He just thought her rebellious stage would've ended by now.

He took a step into the light and their eyes met through the glass, but this time she didn't cower to the back office. Instead, she looked straight at him and mouthed, *go home.*

CHAPTER THREE

Cathy fought the urge to follow Devon West with her eyes as he walked across the street. Did he get in a car to leave? Or was he still only a few feet away? A tingle vibrated up the back of her neck, telling her he was still there, in the distance, so she returned her attention to Judy, afraid he could see her watching him.

"Okay, spill it," Judy demanded. "What's up with Mr. Sexy?"

Cathy huffed. "What are you talking about? He's a stranger in town and is interested in our new barista back there. You know darn well I love this town, and I'm not about to let any outsider stir up trouble."

Judy eyed her for a moment then retrieved a little black pouch from her purse, slid out a wooden circle that had a gold hook attached to it and set it on the edge of the table. The metal hook hung down and she slipped the strap of her handbag onto the hook.

Cathy rolled her eyes. The woman had more gadgets than a dog had fleas. Couldn't she have just hung her purse on the back of her chair like everyone else?

"Trouble?" Judy asked. "Like what?"

"Beats me. All I know is he's in here, eyeing a young woman. Perhaps he's another Ted Bundy. You know, all suave and handsome. He uses his charms to lure you out and then *whamo*." Cathy slapped the side of one hand against the palm of the other like an axe to accentuate her point.

Judy quirked an eyebrow. "So, you admit he's handsome."

Cathy shook her head. "Did you not hear me? He could be some serial killer or rapist or something. He just needs to leave town."

"Uh-huh," Judy said, nodding as though she was placating a toddler.

"Oh no, you don't. Whatever wild idea you've got in that head of yours, you need to get rid of it this instant. You're not setting me up on any more dates. You convinced me to go meet that man in Knoxville and it turned into a horror show. No way. Not going to happen. I'm not taking any more of your insane advice. I'm the matchmaker of this town, not you."

"So, it didn't go well?" Judy reached across the table to grip her hand. "I'm so sorry, hon."

Judy's sorrowful eyes filled her with guilt. "I don't need your sympathy. I just need you to leave the matchmaking to me."

Judy held up her hands. "Okay, I'm sorry. But tell me what happened."

Cathy shook her head. "You said you had news on Amelia."

Judy sighed. "Yes."

This time Cathy reached across the table to take

her friend's hand. "What is it? Did the tests reveal anything?"

Judy squeezed her hand as if she never wanted to let it go. It warmed Cathy's heart to be able to be there for her best friend, especially after all the mistakes she'd made. "We don't know for sure, but James is taking me to the hospital in the morning to be with them when they do the scans."

Cathy slid her coffee to the side, ignoring the tempting aroma of peppermint. "Scans for what?"

Judy took a long breath. "They believe there's something more seriously wrong now. She's losing weight and not doing well regardless of what they try. They're going to look for tumors and..." Judy shuddered.

"It's okay. I'm here." Cathy squeezed her hand and leaned closer, trying to reassure her friend that she'd be there for her through anything.

"Amelia could have cancer." Judy's hands trembled.

"Oh, darling. I'm so sorry." Without letting go of Judy's hand, she straightened in her chair. "Listen, I'll go pack a bag and stay at the farm tonight then I can ride up with you and be there to help any way I can."

Judy shook her head and that look she always gave right before she tried to gracefully wiggle out of something appeared. "That won't be necessary."

Cathy sighed. "I get it. You need to be with family. I'm overstepping again."

Judy stood and opened her arms, pulling Cathy into a hug. "Girl, you are family."

Cathy held her skinny best friend tight. "You tell me what you need and I'll be there. Anything. Anytime of the day. Until you tell me what you need, I'll remain out of it."

Judy leaned back. "You? Stay out of it? Ha. We both know that's not going to happen. You can't help yourself, dear. But I love you for it. And I know it's because you care."

Cathy took her seat once more. "If I promise my best friend I'll stay on the sidelines, that's what I'll do. You may not be able to teach old dogs new tricks but I can still learn."

Judy chuckled. "Hey, can I have a sip of that? It smells delicious."

"Sure. Do you want a London Fog?" Cathy reached for her purse.

"No, thanks. I already had three cups of tea today. I've been stress drinking." She laughed, took a sip and returned it to Cathy. "So, tell me about your date."

Figuring her pride was a small price to pay to help keep Judy's mind off her poor grandbaby struggling in the hospital, Cathy sighed. "Where to start?" She took a sip of her mocha. "But this is just between us, mind you."

Judy crossed her heart then held her hand up, palm forward. "I won't breathe a word...except to maybe James and Lisa." When Cathy shook her head, she said with a chuckle, "Hey, we need some form of entertainment around here."

Cathy leaned back in her chair, taking her mocha with her. "When I arrived at the hotel in Knoxville, I discovered he'd only booked one room." *Scumbag*. "I quickly reserved a second room, which cost me a fortune since it was last minute, and then went to dress for dinner."

Judy leaned her elbow on the table, covering her mouth with her hand. No doubt in preparation to hide her laughter. "Did you wear the new one with the lace bodice?"

Cathy nodded. "I did. Crammed myself into that girdle thing then put on that ridiculously expensive dress to go priss around like a peacock looking for a mate."

Judy laughed. "Stop. You look beautiful in it and you know it."

For a second, she had thought so as well, but after seeing the man's face drop, she realized she'd been kidding herself.

"What happened when you went to meet him for dinner?" Judy asked.

"What didn't happen. First, he lied on his profile. I mean, he sent me a picture of an entirely different person. Now, I'll admit I wouldn't have been immediately attracted to the man in front of me, but I'm not shallow. I would've gotten to know him online then gone to meet him anyway if he seemed nice. I'm not one to go for looks. I just want compatibility. But to find he had completely lied, that made me angry."

Judy opened her mouth to say something, but Cathy pushed her cup back across the table. "Here. Drink the rest. And before you say anything, I know I'm the pot calling the kettle black. I lied about my weight.

I'm a cow compared to what's on my profile, but at least I sent him a real picture. Okay, it was only of my face, but still."

Judy shook her head. "I was just going to say how wrong it was to send you such a picture. And you're not a cow. As a matter of fact, I've been wanting to ask you what you've been doing. I think you've thinned out even more since I saw you a week ago. When I hugged you, I realized how much you've lost. You should be proud."

Cathy hadn't thought about it in the last few days, but she actually hadn't been craving comfort food like normal. Usually when something went wrong, she would binge on junk food. "Thanks, but he didn't think so. After he recovered from the shock, he pulled out my chair then scooted his to the other side of the table to get as far away from me as he could."

Judy took a drink of coffee. "How rude."

"That's what I thought, so of course, you know me. I went on the offensive. I immediately called him out on the hotel room issue. We'd agreed ahead of time he would book two rooms. I told him I had no way of knowing if he was a psychopath or a gentleman."

"Smart," Judy agreed.

"Well," Cathy huffed, "he said it was a mistake and that if he had known I was such a classy lady he wouldn't have invited me for an overnight stay." She rolled her eyes. "His eyes barely left my chest. Then he said, 'You're not what I expected.'"

"No," Judy gasped. "He didn't."

"He did. Oh, but that's not all. Then it went from

bad to horrible. I told him he had grossly misrepresented himself and asked if the picture he'd sent was from two decades ago or straight from a magazine."

Judy laughed. "Good for you. What did he say?"

"He said I shouldn't be so superficial and that at my age, I should do it with the lights off. Then he went on to tell me he had a *lot* more to offer despite the lack of hair on his head."

"No," Judy breathed.

"Yes. Well, I'm afraid I lost it at that point. I'd never been so humiliated. I mean, getting dressed up and driving all the way to Knoxville for a date with a complete stranger that I met over the internet. I don't think I was as mad at him as I was at myself." She sighed. "I knew internet dating wasn't for me. Heck, dating in general isn't for me, but I thought for a second..."

"You thought what?" Judy brushed her thumb up and down Cathy's arm.

She shook her head. "It doesn't matter." How could Cathy confess, even to her best friend, that she'd never felt wanted a day in her life? Her kids had all left the minute they could and her husband had been more of a roommate who never noticed she was even in the room.

On the drive up yesterday, she'd actually considered going back to scumbag's room with him, if only to feel wanted for a few minutes.

"You can tell me," Judy nudged.

"Oh, I'll tell you all right. I picked up that little handbag you convinced me to buy and walloped him over the head with it."

"Good for you," Judy beamed. "I hope there was something heavy in it though."

Cathy shrugged. "I might've hit him with the handle of my hairbrush. It's small but it made quite the thump. Unfortunately, it also caused everyone to stare at us."

Judy quirked an eyebrow. "So? Since when do you care about that?"

"I don't usually, but when I turned to leave, my heel caught in the table cloth and I tripped. Not just a tumble, mind you. My legs went over my head, my hip slammed into another table and food flew everywhere." Cathy let her head drop into her hands. "It was mortifying."

"Oh, darling. I'm so sorry." Judy stroked her hair. "If it's any consolation, it was his loss. You really do look fantastic."

"Thank you," Cathy mumbled.

"Hey, chin up. If nothing else, this has motivated you to start taking care of yourself. Not only do you look hot, but I get to keep my best friend for a lot longer. I was starting to worry about your health, but now you look twenty years younger and more fit than a thirty-year-old."

Cathy lifted her head. "You're just trying to make me feel better."

"Since when do I care about making you feel better?" Judy laughed. "I'm here to tell you how it is. So, let me tell you. You might be gun-shy after what happened, but no matter what, your next date has to go better than this one."

"Gee, thanks." Cathy rolled her eyes.

"Seriously. Didn't you notice that man was checking you out?" Judy pointed to the table where she'd been sitting with Devon. "His eyes were just about to bulge out of his head. Trust me. I know that look. Besides, he's handsome."

"Yes, and full of himself. I mean, did you not just hear me swear off dating forever?"

Judy clapped her hands together. "I've heard this before. Do you remember after prom?"

"Don't even say it." Cathy waved her hands in front of Judy. "I still can't talk about it to this day." Memories of her prom dress ripping as she fell down a flight of stairs outside her date's home gouged the already open wound in her soul. "Nope, still can't talk about that."

"Maybe not, but you met Sam that next weekend after you had sworn off men, remember? Poor guy had to be your friend for six months before you'd agree to date him, but it all worked out."

Had it really? She had been friends with her late husband, and that was all they ever were. They didn't have an epic love and she'd been okay with that. She didn't have the stomach for it then and she wanted nothing to do with it now. "I'm too old for all this. I like the clothes and how I feel, but I'll just keep doing it for me."

"I think that's a good attitude." Judy smiled and took her purse from the table, flipping the little object back together and sliding it inside her bag. "For now."

"You listen here, Judy Gaylord Benjamin. You're not a matchmaker and you shouldn't play around with such nonsense. It's a complicated and dangerous game that should be left up to us professionals."

Judy stood with a huff. "You'd think you'd put together every couple in town."

"I have...almost. I managed to get you and James back together, didn't I?"

Judy cocked her hip, resting her hand on it. "Yeah, after forty years. I don't think I can work that slow. In another forty years, we'll both be dead."

"Speak for yourself." Cathy rose and matched Judy's stance.

"Fine, I'm not going to fight with you. Just don't let a good thing pass you by because you're being stubborn, or because you jumped to silly conclusions."

"I'm not stubborn and I don't jump to conclusions," Cathy shot back.

Judy shook her head. "You know I love you, but you're a stubborn old mule that won't listen to reason."

"Now, I'm not only old, but I'm also a mule? Got any more insults you'd like to swing at your *BFF*?"

"Yeah. Stop running from any man that pays you a compliment and let go of the past. Oh, and wait by the phone, because I might need your crazy stubbornness to get me through all this business with my grandbaby."

Cathy gave her a rough bear hug. "You got it. I'll come up there and kick you in the tush if you start falling apart. You got that? Lisa and Eric need you, so hold it together."

"Yes, ma'am." Judy wiped away a stray tear.

"Thank you. And Cathy?"

"Yeah?"

Judy shuffled backward toward the door. "I really do just want you to be happy. You might not believe me, but you deserve it."

Before Cathy could open her mouth to argue, Judy skedaddled out the door.

The café had cleared out some, with the shops closing for the night. Funny how only twenty-four hours earlier she had butterflies in her stomach and felt alive for the first time in years. Now, she stood in the middle of a nearly empty coffee shop, reluctant to go home to an empty house. Well, until Trianna returned sometime around midnight to sleep before leaving again first thing in the morning. She hadn't even seen her temporary roommate in almost three days, except for their quick chat earlier in the coffee shop.

"Can I get you anything else?" Becca asked, wiping down the table behind her.

"Yes. You can tell me why you were hiding from that man."

"I wasn't—"

"Don't even try it. You ran away faster than a bee stung stallion."

Becca scrubbed at a non-existent spot on the table. "He's a relative."

"Relative? What kind of relative?"

"He's my father," Becca answered nonchalantly, as if talking about the weather.

The thought of that man being married with kids tied a knot in Cathy's belly. Keeping her voice as neutral as possible, she asked, "Where's your mom?"

"Doesn't matter." Becca hunched over further and wiped down a chair. "I'm not going back."

"It does matter," Cathy protested. Feeling selfish, she tried one more time to gain the tidbit of information she just had to know. "Your mother's probably worried sick about you, child."

"I'm not a child, and my mother isn't at home. She's gone."

"Gone?" Cathy bowed her head in shame. The poor child had lost her mother and all she wanted to know was if her father was married. *What kind of person am I?* It didn't even matter. She wanted nothing to do with that man, or any other man ever again. "I'm sorry."

"Nothing to be sorry about. I'm nineteen, on my own, and I prefer it that way." Becca moved to another chair. "Let it go, okay?"

"Sure, hon. Whatever you want." Cathy eyed the thin girl, with her tattoos, and thought about why she would hide from her own father. Was he abusive? A drunk? Too controlling? Why would she leave home to come to this town to work in a coffee shop? There had to be more to the story.

She remembered seeing excitement in Devon's eyes when he thought he'd seen his daughter. She needed more information before she knew what to do. She'd find Devon and question him tomorrow. If he was a good father, with a lost teenage daughter, she'd help him. And if he was some sort of scoundrel, she'd save Becca from him. She couldn't turn her back on someone that needed help. Even if they didn't understand how much they needed it.

CHAPTER FOUR

Devon dropped onto the plush bed inside his room at the Hatfield Inn. He lifted his iPad from the nightstand and leaned back against the headboard, scanning through pictures of Becca when she was a child. Why did they have to grow up? She'd been so precious, beautiful, talented, and loving but then everything changed when she turned thirteen.

The dim lamplight cast a golden glow over the screen, making it difficult to see, so he placed the device back on the nightstand, flicked off his shoes and snatched the folder from his briefcase. Once settled back in bed, he flipped through the document trail that led him to Creekside. Why did Becca city hop from New York to Tennessee over the past few months? Did she think she'd make it big on Broadway but when it didn't happen she came to hide here instead of coming home? So many questions. If she'd just talk to him, perhaps he could help.

His cell phone buzzed and an unfamiliar number appeared on the screen. It buzzed a few more times then went to voice mail. Then he noticed the area code on the brochure for Café Bliss and realized the call was from a local number. His heart soared at the thought of Becca calling him. He quickly dialed the number and waited anxiously to hear his sweet little girl's voice.

"Hello?" answered a woman with a deep southern twang.

"Yes, um. I thought perhaps this was my daughter. Did you just call my phone?" Devon asked.

"Yes, I did."

That voice. It sounded familiar. "Cathy?"

"You remembered my name. How nice."

"Um, I'm not sure how you got my number, but I think you might have gotten the wrong idea."

A *harrumph* sounded from the other end of the line. "Don't flatter yourself, playboy. I'm not calling you for a hook-up."

"Hook up? What are we, sixteen?" Devon teased.

Cathy cleared her throat. "Even at sixteen, I wasn't gullible enough to fall for a man like you. Now, listen up."

For some reason his mouth snapped shut. No woman had ever commanded him to do something. Usually they scooted around the topic, hinted, or asked politely. It drove him nuts that they wouldn't just get to the damn point already.

"Good, now that you stopped talking perhaps you'll hear me. First, I got your number from Mrs. Hatfield."

"So you called the inn to track me down?" Great, he'd hit on a crazy woman. "Seriously, it was just casual flirting. I didn't mean to give you the wrong idea."

"Get over yourself already. I didn't think I was anything special to you. Besides, I know your type, hitting on anything with two legs. If you'd stop thinking every woman fell for your crap then maybe you'd be quiet long enough to discuss your daughter with me."

He bolted from the bed. "You know?"

"Yes, I know, but I have some questions you need to answer first. Meet me at the diner tomorrow morning at eight A.M. Don't be late. You'll buy me breakfast and answer my questions. Got it?"

"Should I bring flowers, too?"

"You only do that for special dates. And this isn't a date. It'll be a lesson in manners and a chance for me to figure out what you're doing here. Show up, or don't. I don't really care." The phone clicked off before he could rebut. The woman was a walking fireball.

He paced the floor and eyed his phone. He wanted to call her back and order her to tell him why she was hiding his daughter from him, but something told him the woman wouldn't budge once she made up her mind. He took off his shirt and trousers and climbed into bed. It was early, but he'd had a long day trying to locate Becca, even with the new information from his private investigator.

He tossed and turned for hours until he finally fell into a fitful sleep. At around six in the morning, he rolled out of bed and put on some running clothes. He needed a stress release before he faced the questions that had been plaguing him for the past two years.

Why had Becca runaway? And why didn't she want to see him?

He tiptoed down the stairs and out into the street, leaving the front door how he'd found it—unlocked.

Apparently, a legendary relative of the Hatfield clan could handle herself and didn't need to secure her inn at night.

The morning was cold and damp. His joints ached, but he knew by the end of the run he'd feel better. It was a quiet street, not a car in sight until about halfway down Main. The lights flipped on in the bakery just as he passed by. When he reached the café he looked through the window, hoping to catch a glimpse of Becca making coffee. Perhaps he could even go in and order some, try to hear her voice for the first time in over a year. Unfortunately, he only spotted Mrs. Fletcher, so he kept going, planning to return later.

His feet pounded against the pavement with a rhythmic thumping. His right shoulder, left big toe and low back ached, but he ran through the pain. Getting old sucked, but the thought of slowing down as age crept up on him only made him run harder. With a good pace, he continued past the businesses and found himself on a quiet residential road. Old-fashioned homes dotted the tree-lined street every few hundred feet. Some remained dark, so all he could see was the picket fence bordering their lawns, or their silhouettes.

The fourth house on the right was a beautiful Victorian and his legs stopped moving. The awe of the classic home kept him running in place for a few seconds as he eyed the intricate detail illuminated by the front porch light. It was the kind of home Kimmie and he had dreamed of when they married. The white picket fence fantasy with tons of children and a happy-ever-after kind of love, but that wasn't to be reality.

A dog barked in the distance, drawing him from his memories, and he ran on, yet his mind's eye remained outside that home. It was perfect, the home from his dreams. Not the sterile track house they'd lived in back in Connecticut.

After three miles, he found himself back on Main Street and walked along the shops. The florist had opened her doors and set out buckets of flowers and potted poinsettias. The café was now lit up as well. People began to pull into the angled parking spaces to grab their morning fix. He walked past the inn and continued to Café Bliss, but remained on the opposite side of the street. He felt like he was hunting a scared little rabbit, afraid it would hop back into its hole at the first sign of the hunting dog.

At the edge of a building, he found the shadowy spot where he stood the night before, giving him a clear view of the counter inside the coffee house. He held his breath, willing the man ordering to move so he could see who was working. Headlights flashed across him, so he turned and faded back against the wall. Once the car was gone, he returned to his spot and caught sight of his daughter.

For a moment, he thought just catching a glimpse would be enough, but his heart ached to go hug her, speak to her, to be a family again. But the way she'd looked at him the night before warned him he needed a plan, maybe even some reinforcements.

Cathy.

He'd known her less than twenty-four hours but had no doubt she was a woman who could change minds and make things happen.

With one more glance, he etched Becca's image into his mind then returned to the inn for a hot shower and a change of clothes. After he dressed in dark slacks and a white dress shirt, he decided to tiptoe down the stairs, willing Mrs. Hatfield to still be asleep.

When he reached the bottom of the stairs, every light was on. He could hear soft music playing from the parlor and the aroma of strong coffee drifted from the kitchen. *This isn't going to be easy.* Besides himself, there was only one couple staying in the inn, so he knew she'd come looking for him.

Before he could slip quietly to the front door, Mrs. Hatfield teetered around the corner on her cane. "There you are. I already have the Smiths settled in the kitchen for some breakfast. Why don't you join us?" She wobbled but he resisted the urge to offer her a seat. He'd learned the hard way yesterday that she considered such assistance an insult.

"Thank you so much, but I'm meeting someone for breakfast this morning."

Mrs. Hatfield moved to his side and nudged his hip with her elbow. "Who ya meetin'?"

"A Ms. Cathy Mitchell," he replied, but suspected she already knew since she gave Cathy his number last night.

"Oh, yes. Well, she told me last night she lost your number and that she needed to reach you. So, I obliged her request. You look awful nice for a business meeting, though."

He glanced down at his clothes. "This is how I

always dress. Is there something wrong with it?"

"Shoot. What do I know? For a second, I thought maybe you two had a date. How silly is that?" She chuckled, a dry, dusty sound almost like a cackle.

"Why's that silly?" He regretted asking before the words even left his lips, but it was too late now. He could already see the delight in Mrs. Hatfield's eyes.

"She doesn't date. Not since she lost her husband some years back. Not many men can handle her. She's got a fire in her belly, that one. Sometimes, I think she is a distant relative of those Hatfields." She gestured with her head toward the fireplace mantel in the parlor. "Have I shown you the picture?"

"Yes. I saw it last night. They looked like a tough group." And they did, too. Even the children had posed for the picture with shotguns.

She chuckled. "Yep. My kin is a tough bunch."

Devon noticed the sun, now shining down on the street outside. "Well, I better go. Thanks for the offer of breakfast, though. Perhaps another day."

"Tomorrow it is then. I'll make plenty. Be downstairs at seven-thirty sharp. Enjoy." She hobbled off faster than a receiver running for a touchdown.

He shook his head. *That woman isn't nearly as weak as she makes out.*

Before she had a chance to change her mind and tie him to the sofa, he took off out the front door. At the bottom of the steps, he spotted the floral shop a few doors down and smiled inwardly. *She did say something about flowers*, he thought, and he still had fifteen minutes to kill before meeting her. Perhaps it would start things off on a good note, maybe ease some of her animosity. If she relaxed, she might be willing to help him out with his daughter. Becca clearly didn't want to talk to him, so enlisting someone else's help was the best chance he had of reconnecting with her.

He waltzed up the front walk of the florist shop and eyed the different buckets of flowers. Avoiding the red roses, or any roses for that matter, he chose a sweet bouquet of fall colors. They were lovely and he figured anyone would appreciate the gesture.

He tugged on the front door, but it was still locked, so he tapped on the glass. A moment later, a woman in her mid-twenties came to the door.

"Can I help you, sir?"

"Yes. I'd like to purchase these." He held up the arrangement.

"Those are lovely. Good choice. Will you be paying by cash, check, or credit card?" the woman asked.

"Credit card."

"In that case, go ahead and take them. My machine isn't working right now, so you can stop by later to pay if that works for you."

He stood there eyeing the woman, waiting for her to change her mind, or tell him she was just kidding. "Are you sure?"

"Yes, sir. You look like an honest person. Go ahead."

"Okay. Thank you." He nodded, but still expected her to scream that he'd stolen them after he made it down the block.

As he turned away, she shut the door, but left it

unlocked. *How can she stay in business if she allows people to take flowers and not pay?* Did everyone in town always come back and settle their bills?

Still mulling over small town life, he walked right up to the diner before realizing it. He pulled open the door and stood for a moment, blinking at the glaring lights.

"Good morning, sir," a passing waitress called. "Take a seat wherever you like."

He found a booth at the front, by the windows, and slid into the seat. Something sizzled on the large grill behind the breakfast counter and the aroma of fresh baked bread made his stomach growl.

"What can I get for you?" the waitress asked.

"Coffee for now, please. I'm waiting for someone."

"Sure. Coming right up."

Devon laid the flowers on the table then fixed his gaze on the doorway so he could see when Cathy entered. Feeling his phone buzz in his pocket, he retrieved it and found a missed call. He checked the voicemail but there was none. The call log showed some generic eight-hundred number. As he slipped the phone back into his pocket, a gust of wind blew in and he looked up expecting to find Cathy. Instead, he spotted Becca.

His heart pounded in his chest. *Is she here to talk to me?* He scooted out and stood next to the table, willing her to run to him with open arms and ask to come home. Finally, after two years of searching for her she was standing only feet away.

"Becca?" he choked, opening his arms to welcome

her back into his life. He didn't care why she'd left or where she'd been, he just wanted his baby girl back. He held his breath, waiting for her to move, to say something.

Ignoring him, she faced the lady behind the counter. "I heard you weren't feeling well. I thought I'd stop in and see if you wanted me to take the afternoon shift so you could go home early. Mrs. Fletcher said she could spare me after the morning rush."

"Oh, darling. That would put you in for a double, plus the morning at Café Bliss. You're going to make yourself sick. Aren't you taking on too much? You shouldn't be working two jobs as it is."

"I'll be fine." She didn't give the woman a chance to argue. Instead, she marched up to Devon, crossed her arms over her chest and glared at him.

"Becca, honey. I've missed you. I don't know why you're here, but I just want to be part of your life again. Please. You don't have to work so hard. I know you weren't happy living in our house, so I sold it. We can move anywhere. It doesn't matter as long as we're together. We're a family."

Her eyes narrowed. "Family? You don't know what family is. Leave."

Devon reached for his daughter's frail arm. She'd lost so much weight and dark circles shadowed her eyes. "Please, I've been trying to find you. Why did you run when I found you in New York?"

Becca dropped her arms to her sides and lifted her chin. "Just go back to Connecticut before you ruin everything *again*."

CHAPTER FIVE

Cathy brushed past the potted fern adorned with tiny Christmas ornaments outside of J & L Antiques. It was strange to have the shop closed. She'd call Judy later and offer to open it for her. Being the season for shopping, they needed to be open as much as possible this time of year.

The heavy scents of breakfast coming from the diner had her hesitating. Her stomach was gurgling unhappily and the idea of eating something rich and fatty didn't sit well. Now that she thought about it, she'd forgotten to eat dinner. When was the last time she'd forgotten to eat?

Passing by her reflection outside the florist, she paused and smoothed her jacket out. Twirling a stray curl out of her eyes until it set perfect to the side of her temple, she realized Judy was right. She did look different, and she liked what she saw. Screw men. Who cared what they thought. She checked her teeth for lipstick then sauntered into the diner, ready for a fight. The man she met last night would be a tough nut to crack. Especially with him distracting her all the time with his suave moves.

As the door swung shut behind her, Mrs. Heller waved from the breakfast counter. "Hi ya, Cathy."

Cathy smiled and waved back. "Good morning. How you feeling? Someone mentioned you were under the weather."

"It's nothing serious." Mrs. Heller leaned over the counter. "Bladder infection again. I'm just uncomfortable but Doc said he could see me this afternoon."

"Let me know if you need anything. I can bring you food, beverages, or company anytime you want."

"Thanks, darling. You want something special this morning?"

Cathy shook her head. "No, thanks. I'll go for a cup of tea, though."

"You got it. Coming right up."

Cathy scanned the few patrons quietly eating until she spotted a man with salt and pepper hair slumped over a table, flowers wrapped in green tissue paper by his side. *Are those for me?* She scooted closer and decided it really was Devon West. A couple of feet from the table she cleared her throat.

He lifted his head and gave a weak smile. "Hi. How are you?" His expression solemn, he stood and took her hand.

"You can skip the kiss. What's going on?" she asked, scooting into the seat across from him. "You look like you just lost your last worm while trying to catch your dinner."

"What?" Devon's eyebrows wrinkled then he shook his head and sat down again.

45

"Never mind. Let's just have a chat for a bit." She couldn't help but eye the flowers. She hadn't gotten flowers since...1974? Before she'd married Sam.

"Here's a peace offering. I saw them when I went for a run this morning and thought of you."

Cathy smiled, unsure of how to accept such a gesture. Her husband had never been the romantic type. His idea of romance was to put the toilet seat down so she didn't fall in at night. She sniffed the bouquet, the fresh scent of flowers mixing with the autumn fragrances of cinnamon and apple. "I thought this wasn't a social occasion. Be careful, Mr. West. You might cause me to think this is a date. You wouldn't want to give me the wrong idea now, would you?"

He smiled and the desperation that had plagued his eyes settled into more of a soft puppy dog look. "Why don't we order something to eat?" Devon gestured to her menu.

Mrs. Heller arrived with a small silver teapot, cup, and an assortment of teabags. "Here you go, Cathy. Do you two want anything else?"

Devon looked to Cathy.

"Not right now," she said. "I'm gonna just have tea."

Mrs. Heller's face grew stern. "You're gonna waste away if you skip any meals. You look light as a feather now."

Her hand shook and she had to concentrate on not dropping the small teapot as she poured boiling water into her teacup. No one had ever told her she was light before. Well, not since before having kids in the late

1970s.

Devon picked up his menu then handed it to Mrs. Heller. "I'd like some oatmeal and more coffee, please."

"Coming right up."

"So, I'm here. What's so important?" Devon asked as Mrs. Heller returned to the kitchen.

Cathy shifted the bouquet over further and picked up her cup to take a sip. "The woman you were stalking yesterday."

"Stalking?" Devon laughed aloud, his voice booming with mirth, while Cathy calmly sipped her tea.

"I'm not a stalker, I promise. You've got this all wrong."

"Do I?" She quirked an eyebrow.

"Yes. She's my daughter." Devon pushed his cup to the end of the table as Mrs. Heller approached, but Cathy knew he was just buying time to collect himself.

"If she's your daughter, why would she be hiding from you?" Cathy asked.

"I wish I knew." Devon's smile faded.

"I don't understand. How can you not know why she doesn't want to see or speak to you?"

Devon leaned back and rubbed his chin. "Well, because her mother took off and then she took off. Both without a word."

"Cheater?" Cathy blurted before she thought better of it.

Devon gripped his mug and narrowed his gaze. "Never."

Cathy shrugged and straightened her red scarf. "You can't blame me for drawing that conclusion.

You're a player if I ever met one."

He leaned forward as if sniffing his coffee and hovered there for a moment. "I've never cheated on anyone in my life. I'm all talk. Really."

Cathy studied the man's movements. He didn't look so cocky now. "So, you're just a huge flirt that toys with a lady's emotions? Even worse."

Devon sighed. "No. I don't know why, but I guess I started to date women after she left for company, but I didn't want them to stick around."

Cathy huffed. "Well, that's nice. So, you are a player."

Devon reached across the table and grabbed her hand. "No. That's just it, I'm not. I mean, the women I've been with weren't looking for a relationship either. They just wanted romance and sex. It was a fair trade between two consenting adults."

"You make it sound like a business proposal," Cathy said. This man's words churned her stomach, but the expression on his face softened her heart. "So, you dated out of loneliness, but your heart was too broken to connect with anyone after your wife left?"

Devon shrugged. "I guess I never thought of it that way."

"It makes sense. Do you still see your ex?" Cathy asked, her curiosity getting the better of her.

"No. I haven't seen her since the day she walked out the door. She just gave up on Becca and me. Said she couldn't live a lie anymore, packed a bag and ran out. I tried to find her, but I couldn't. It wasn't until a year later that divorce papers arrived."

"Did you see her in court?"

Devon glanced around the restaurant, his eyes stopping on the window beside their booth. She knew he was watching the coffee shop where his daughter had the morning shift. Perhaps the man wasn't that bad. Maybe he just wanted to make things right.

"No. The papers stated that she was leaving everything to us and that she just wanted to disappear. Of course, there wasn't much left. She'd cleaned out all our accounts before she disappeared."

Cathy squeezed his hand. "So, you let her go without any information or retribution? I don't know if I could do that. I'd probably want to put her on trial to find out the truth, or to shame her or something. You're a better person than I."

"I didn't do it for me. I did it for Becca. She was all I had left and she started acting out after her mother abandoned us. I learned quickly a girl needs a mother, but I couldn't bring myself to marry again, or even date anyone more than a few times. I guess we both felt abandoned."

The way his voice cracked with sorrow made Cathy's heart soften.

"I let her go because I didn't want Becca to be put through any more than she had. I wanted to protect my little girl from more heartbreak. At least, that's what I told myself."

Cathy rubbed a finger across his knuckles, attempting to comfort him. "How did she take it after the divorce?"

"Not good. That's when she disappeared for a few

days and returned home drunk, with *love* tattooed across her knuckles. She accused me of driving her mother away and blamed me for not going to court and facing her to make her come home."

"Sounds like how most young girls would act. I mean, both of you have suffered a great loss, never hearing from the woman again."

"I said I never saw her again. She did call once, and I tried to find out why she left, but she ranted about things that didn't make sense."

Mrs. Heller returned with a bowl of warm oatmeal and set it to the side. When she eyed their joined hands, they both pulled away.

Cathy sat back in her seat, refusing to make eye contact with Mrs. Heller. She didn't want to invite conversation. Not when she was about to find out why he was here and if she should help or run him out of town.

"So, you still don't know why?" Cathy asked.

"No. She said that we were never a family and that I fooled myself into thinking we were. She said she only married me because of Becca and she couldn't stand the guilt anymore. She was tired of living a false, mundane life and she needed to find herself."

"That's awful. I'm sorry." Cathy sipped her tea, enjoying the warm liquid sliding down her throat. "You're daughter's nineteen, right? Most kids have left home by then. So, why are you here? What do you hope to do?"

Devon gazed out the window once more. "I hoped to reconnect with my daughter. Ask her why she left. I let her mother go without a fight, but I can't do that again. Not with my little girl. She's all I have left." He chuckled weakly. "I'm not sure why I'm telling you all this."

Cathy smiled. "Yes, you do. You're hoping I'm going to help you get closer to your daughter. That's why you brought the flowers, put on the charm and showed fake interest in me." Her words stung and she knew it. A part of her had hoped he was interested, but now she saw it was all a play.

Devon reached across the table again, offering his hand. "Cathy, I didn't mean..."

Cathy kept her hands in her lap. "It's fine. Trust me. I never fell for it for a second." She quickly took another sip of tea to keep herself from tearing up. *Blasted emotions.*

"Listen, can we start again? I'm afraid I've been playing this game with women for so long I'm not sure how to be myself anymore." Devon scooted the flowers toward her. "Please. I want you to have these flowers. I may not have bought them with proper sincerity, but I can honestly say there isn't a woman I've met in the last few years that I'd want to give flowers to more than you. I'm sure you're used to getting flowers all the time, and it was probably a pathetic move, but I'd still like to give them to you. Will you accept them?" He smiled, his eyebrows raised in question.

"Sure, I'll take them. To be honest, I haven't received flowers in years. They'll look nice on my kitchen table."

"Really? I find that hard to believe. What about

your husband?"

"He passed away a few years ago, but he wasn't the romantic type. I don't think I've gotten flowers for decades." Cathy eyed the floral arrangement once more. "I even tried dropping hints about flowers to my husband once. Told him my favorite flower was an orchid. He looked it up and told me I was crazy, that it was a bloom on a stick and cost a fortune. He was a practical man. A good provider, great friend and fantastic life partner, but not the sensitive type."

Devon pulled his oatmeal closer and Cathy leaned back to take her hand away, but he tightened his grasp. "I have another one I can use to eat with." He winked, sending a tingle of excitement down her back. "Certainly, he took you out for nice dinners or romantic vacations."

"We went to Alabama once for a football game with a bunch of friends, and up to the mountains to go fishing a few times." A hint of guilt nibbled at her desire to be around this man, like she was betraying her husband's memory. "He was the best husband anyone could ask for. Strong, hardworking, and treated me with respect."

Devon dipped his spoon into the oatmeal. "I guess that's something."

Cathy couldn't hold back her defensive tongue. "You make it sound like my husband didn't love me because he didn't shower me with jewelry, flowers, and chocolates, but I can assure you he did." Her voice wavered with her doubts, the ones that had plagued her throughout her marriage. Was she just a baby factory and live-in maid? She cared for him, but was there really so little love in their marriage? Every time one of her friends bragged about what their husbands gave them she'd roll her eyes and say how frivolous it was, but deep down she'd have done anything for Sam to give her one gift from the heart.

"I have no doubt. I'm glad he was good to you." Devon plastered a smile on his face, his tone changing. "Love is shown in so many different ways. Tell me. If you could ask your husband today if he'd do something with you or give you a gift, what would it be?"

"What a silly question," Cathy scoffed, taking another sip of her tea.

Devon ate a few bites of his oatmeal then dabbed at his cheeks with his napkin. "Is it? If I were still married, I'd ask my wife to go on a hike to enjoy the fall leaves or maybe picnic at a beautiful spot in the country."

"That sounds nice." Cathy smiled, one that lit her soul. Then she sighed. "There are so many little things I'd love to do."

"Like what?" Devon nudged.

She shrugged. "Take a walk through town in the evening, hand in hand, looking in the shop windows and enjoying the Christmas music. Or sit in front of the fire and talk about a book or just read quietly, enjoying each other's company. Sip hot chocolate while sitting on my front porch, watching the kids all bundled up playing in the street. Go to church with me, or watch old movies." She eyed him, wanting to share her deepest desire, but how silly would that be. She'd never even told her best friend about how she wanted to travel before. "I'd love to go some place far away," she managed.

"Where?" Devon pushed.

Cathy sighed. "You'll think I'm crazy."

He shook his head. "No more than I already do."

She smacked his hand, splattering oatmeal all over the table. They both laughed, relaxing the mood between them.

He wiped it up with his napkin and met her gaze. "Tell me."

"Paris," she said finally. "Could you imagine? With my accent? They'd think I was some dumb country bumpkin."

"Is there anything specific you'd want to see in Paris?" Devon set the soiled napkin to the side then took a few more from the metal dispenser at the end of the table.

"The Louvre. I used to draw years ago. Nothing great, but deep down I'd always wanted to go to art school. Since that wasn't to be, I guess I wanted to revel in the beautiful art from the Renaissance greats."

"I could see you being an artist," Devon said. "Do you still draw? I'd love to see your work."

"My work? Oh, no. No one's ever seen my drawings."

"No one?"

"Not a single person. Judy, my late husband, my parents. No one. I'm not that good and people would just laugh. Now, you can't go telling folks I'm some wannabe artist. They'll run you out of town for talking crazy."

"I thought you wanted me gone anyway." Devon's lip curled into a playful grin.

"I did."

"Did?"

Cathy straightened. "Yes. Well, I'm not sure yet if you're the good dad trying to save his daughter or the man who drove her to leave. Until I figure that out, I'm not on your side. Got it?"

"You mean my charm didn't woo you into believing me?"

"Not even close," Cathy chuckled. The man made conversation easy. She didn't feel guarded or defensive, but rather relaxed and connected.

Devon scooped up the last bite of oatmeal then laid the spoon in the bowl. "Well, it sounds like I have a lot to prove. But if you do end up believing me, will you help? I'd like you to try to convince my daughter to talk to me. I can't lose..." He lowered his head.

Cathy's heart lurched at his obvious sorrow. He'd been through so much. That young lady across the street might be a fine worker and a polite young woman. Heck, Mrs. Fletcher had even covered for her, but she had some major convincing to do before Cathy would let her off the hook and send this man out of town.

"I'll keep my mind open to the possibility that you're an okay guy, despite your character flaws," Cathy teased. She retrieved the flowers then scooted to the edge of the bench. "I best be going. I have to make a phone call and I might be working for Judy and Lisa while they're away.

"Well, at least I'll know where to find you." He stood and grabbed her hand, bringing it to his mouth for a kiss.

She fought to ignore that tingle-up-her-arm thing. "You need to stop doing that. I've got your number, you know."

"I guess I'll have to give up my signature move then." He released her hand and for a second, she wanted to retract her words, but then he touched her upper arm and leaned in to kiss her cheek.

Her ankles wobbled and she thought she'd fall off the little heels of her boots. *What does he think he's doing? I should slap him for being so forward,* she thought. What made him think he had the right? But as much as her mind protested, her body didn't agree. Instead of shoving him away, she leaned into him. For a moment, she felt...special.

"Have a good day. I'm going to pop over to the college and check on things. I'll be back this evening. You have my number if anything arises with Becca." He grabbed the check, paid at the register then sauntered out of the diner.

"Wow, Cathy," Mrs. Heller said. "You caught a good one."

Cathy hadn't realized she was even there. But she recovered quickly and swatted her. "Oh, please. There ain't nothing there. He's just playing me for some information, but I'm playing him right back."

"That's not what I saw. He couldn't take his eyes off you." Mrs. Heller cleared the table then carried the dishes to the back, leaving Cathy's mind reeling with possibilities.

But she shook them off and straightened. At the sound of tissue paper crinkling, she glanced down at the flowers in her hand. She'd learned a long time ago that things like romance didn't happen to her. A gypsy at some fool carnival once told her love wasn't in her future. Some women were magnets for passion, others for practicality. Cathy was the practical type, and it was time to go find out Becca's side of the story.

Cathy followed the line of garland strung across the street from the diner to the café. The smells of pine and hazelnut mixed between the Christmas tree lot at the corner and the bakery behind her. This time of year everything smelled and looked beautiful, but it was also the saddest time of year for her. Ever since her kids moved away and her husband died the holiday season was difficult. She'd work the church bizarre, feed the homeless and whatever else she could do to not face Christmas eve at home alone. There was no tree, presents, or children to fill the void in her life, so she tried to fill others.

The coffee shop was nearly empty. "Good morning, Becca. Where is everyone?"

Becca continued to wipe down the counter, not bothering to look up. "The morning rush is usually a little later on shopping days."

"Well, guess we have a few minutes to chat then," Cathy offered before setting her purse on the counter.

Becca froze. "He got to you, didn't he?" She looked up and eyed the flowers in Cathy's hand. "Yep, he sure did."

"Listen, I'm not sure what's going on, but I don't want any drama in my town. Let's just sit and chat for a bit. You tell me why you want your dad to leave and perhaps I can help make that happen. Either way, I just want to help."

Becca eyed her suspiciously then said, "What can I get you?"

Cathy shook her head. "Nothing, I just had tea at the diner."

"You want to talk, I want to get paid." Becca crossed her arms over her chest and narrowed her eyes.

"Fine. Decaf coffee. Leave room for creamer."

Becca slid a paper cup from the stack and walked to the coffee dispenser. Steam coiled above the cup and disappeared into the air. Cathy dropped a couple dollars on the counter and took the cup to the cream station. "Okay. Now, come sit down."

"I don't sit when I'm working." Becca grabbed the rag once more and marched to a table.

Cathy sighed. "Well, if the dwarfs can whistle while they work, you can talk while you wipe tables."

Becca turned her head away, but Cathy still caught her smile. At least the girl wasn't all bad attitude and tattoos.

She plopped the rag down on the table and rested her palms on the top. "Listen, you don't understand my dad's just playing you. It's what he does. Any pretty woman that passes his way, my father will bag in about ten minutes."

Cathy huffed. "I can assure you there will be no

bagging."

Becca tilted her head, her eyebrows raised. "Those flowers from my father?" She sighed. "Yeah, I can see from the look on your face. The same one those other women had. Even the woman my father slept with while still married to my mother. He's a dog and a cheater."

Cathy shook her head. "I can't imagine—"

"That my father would do that to a woman? Let me ask you something. Did he ask you about your dreams or feelings? What makes you happy? Did he touch your hand and make you feel special, like you were the only woman in the room? Trust me, you better run before he ruins you like he did my mother."

Cathy eyed the flowers. She'd pegged him as a player, but for a second, she'd gotten lost in his attention. "Trust me, darling. I can handle myself. Don't you worry about me. Now, tell me. Did you run away because your dad cheated on your mom? Or did your mom leave and it hurt so bad that you left home?"

"Does it matter?" Becca stepped around the table and began wiping down another one.

"Sometimes parents have complications that affect their children. They're not perfect and they make mistakes, but that doesn't mean they love their kids any less. If your mother and father had problems, that doesn't have to ruin you. Talk to your father and explain how he made you feel. He might not have a clue. Adults, especially men, can be clueless at times. And promise me you won't run out of town. Mrs. Fletcher and others in town care about you now. I don't want you breaking their hearts."

Becca's face changed from combative to sorrowful. "I'm not going to run. I can't leave town."

Cathy set the flowers and her purse down on the table. "What's wrong, honey? Are you in some sort of trouble?"

Becca collapsed into a chair and lowered her forehead to the table. "No. It's just that I need to stay here, and my father being here is complicating things. Please, you have to keep him away from me or I'll lose my nerve. After what happened in New York, I can't let this fall apart. I just can't."

Cathy stroked the girl's soft bleached blond hair. "There, there, child. Why can't you leave? What happened in New York?"

"I-I can't tell you. He'll get to you, too. My father has a way of manipulating women. I've witnessed them fall at his feet numerous times."

"Trust me. I'm not that gullible. You need to tell me, or I won't be able to help you."

Beyond the shining tears pooling at the bottom of Becca's eyes, Cathy saw deep sorrow. A grief only someone who'd suffered a great tragedy would understand. "I'm going to regret this, but I'll keep him at a distance for awhile. You need to come clean soon, or I might decide you're just a delinquent that's going to make trouble in my town."

"I promise. I'll be straight. No issues with me." Becca's tears dried a little too quickly, replaced with a devious smile.

Cathy couldn't help feeling she'd just bought a

used car from a greasy man at a makeshift dealership.

CHAPTER SIX

Devon sat at a desk in the musty library of the community college, searching the internet for some sign of his ex-wife. After one meal with Cathy Mitchell, the small town woman with the bright smile, he realized there was more to life then hating his ex for abandoning her family. He'd spent too long trying to forget her. Now, it was time to face her, if for no other reason than to find out why she left and move on with life.

After nearly four hours, he finally admitted defeat. Nothing had come up under her married name or maiden name. Had she died? Gone over seas? Was she living in a convent? He didn't have a clue. The only hint he had was that the divorce papers had been sent by an attorney in Dallas, Texas.

With a headache nagging at his temples and his lower back aching, he decided it was time to turn it over to the private investigator who had located Becca.

Pulling up a new browser, he typed *Creekside* into the search engine. It was time to do a little reconnaissance on the new town his daughter had decided to relocate to. A ton of links popped up for the local paper, news about festivals, awards, and small business owners. After a few clicks, he saw images of the horrible aftermath from what must have been a massive tornado. He clicked on a link that directed him to a photo of the town sheriff, carrying a limp body from the wreckage of a factory. Another of a woman, on her knees crying, with two women by her side trying to assist her. One of them looked like Cathy. It was hard to tell. The woman in the photo didn't appear to have the same frame as the woman he ate breakfast with. Even her hairstyle and clothes looked different. Perhaps Cathy had a sister.

He searched through another few links and found an article about a big child trafficking case being solved by the sheriff. There was a picture of Cathy, standing next to a wrecked Cadillac. He could tell it was Cathy this time, despite her haircut being different. The caption of the picture read *Cathy Mitchell, town hero sacrifices car to take down hit man.*

A hint of pride swelled at the thought of the woman's bravery.

After flipping through several more articles, he realized that Cathy Mitchell regularly fed the hungry, helped rebuild the town after Mother Nature had ripped it apart, and even saved the life of a young woman by ramming her car into the assailant's escape vehicle. He'd suspected there was something special about her, but he hadn't had a clue. This woman was everything his ex-wife had never been. Independent, giving, loving and, more than anything, strong.

For another hour, he read about a woman who

appeared to be more a hero than a small town resident. How could one woman do so much?

Closing the browser windows, he pushed away from the desk and gathered his briefcase. Exiting the building, he tightened his jacket against the evening's damp chill and headed to his car. The drive through backcountry roads allowed him a chance to reflect on his life, mistakes, hopes, and desires. It had been a long time since he thought about anything but finding his daughter and forgetting his ex-wife. Images of Cathy as she'd appeared in the articles replayed in his head during the short forty-five minute drive back to Creekside.

He planned on stopping by the J & L antique store to see Cathy on his way back, just to ask her a few questions about his daughter, but realized she had probably gone home already. The roads were nearly pitch black due to the cloudy, moonless sky. To make matters worse, the backcountry roads twisted and turned, causing him to drive well below the speed limit. Finally, he spotted the Christmas lights in town and loosened his grip on the steering wheel.

Garland stretched from one side of the street to the other and large green, red, and gold balls hung from potted Christmas trees along the sidewalk. Downtown Creekside looked like something from a Hallmark movie, where everything would turn out perfect in the end.

If only I lived in the movies, he thought with a sigh.

He parked his car and made his way to his

shadowy corner to catch a glimpse of his daughter before heading back to the inn. To his disappointment, there was no sign of her. Then he remembered what she'd told the lady at the diner that morning. Leaving his hideout, he walked down the street to the bustling diner.

Becca rushed around the front counter and placed two plates down on a table before hurrying back toward the kitchen. Her bleached hair was pulled back into a ponytail and she wore an apron tied around her small waist.

At a table near the entrance, a woman huffed and turned to her friend. "I guess we won't make our movie."

Becca scrambled to clear another table then ran to the kitchen to pick up an order.

He watched his little girl work so hard. Pride filled him, but so did a desire to help. He spotted a twenty-dollar bill lying on top of the ticket for their meals. "Ma'am? Are you waiting on change?"

She smiled and fluffed her hair before nodding.

"Well, let me see if I can help." He slid his money clip from his pocket and started unfolding the bills. "I can give you all but the coins. Will that work?"

"Certainly, sir. You're a life saver." Her smile turned to disgust. "This girl's struggling," she muttered as she slid the money into her purse without leaving a tip.

He leaned toward her, as though confiding a secret. "I heard she graciously took over for the lady who owns this place because she was ill. It looks like the poor thing's single-handedly running the show. I actually feel bad for her. I think I'll leave her a big tip." He smiled. "You ladies have a good night at the movie." He patted the other lady's shoulder before stepping away and she smiled brightly.

When he reached the counter, he caught the two women throwing a five-dollar bill on the table. *At least Becca didn't get stiffed.* If she was working two jobs, she must need the money. But what for? He picked up the tray with the cash and placed it behind the register then cleared the table and wiped it down.

"Pick up!" the cook yelled out.

A man at the counter looked to the woman beside him. "That's ours. We should be able to eat and make it in time to tuck the kids in before bed."

Devon scooted behind the counter and grabbed the food then served it to the couple. "Here you go. I hope you enjoy."

The man nodded. "Thanks. But you don't look like a waiter."

"I'm just helping out," Devon said, offering another bright smile. "That young lady's working hard."

Another family left a table, so he wiped it down then cleaned off some dirty dishes, placing them in a bin behind the counter.

"Hey. Can I order?"

He turned to find an old man with no teeth seated at the counter. "What would you like, sir?"

"Name's Frank, not *sir*. I'd like some applesauce and some orange juice."

"You got it." Devon wrote it down on a ticket and

clipped it up on the tin rotating thing hanging from the cook's window, hoping he did it right.

Becca stormed at him. "What do you think you're doing back here?"

"I'm helping. It looks like you're short-staffed and could use a hand."

Becca scanned the room. "Fine. But I get the tips and you leave without trying to talk to me once things calm down.

His heart soared to the heavens. This was the first time she'd said more than three words to him since running away. Just the thought of being in the same room with his little girl for a few minutes made him jump to action.

A few more families came in, so he greeted them then sat them at the only open tables after he'd cleared them. "Here you go. I hope you enjoy."

He took another check and this time entered it into the register then ran the card through the machine. It had been years since he worked in a restaurant—more like decades—but it came back quick. For two hours, he waited tables, wiped down surfaces, rang up checks and watched his daughter work hard. The spoiled little girl who'd left home was gone, replaced by a strong, independent young woman. He couldn't have been more proud. He only wished he could be a part of her new life.

The crowd died down until only a few tables remained occupied and he realized how much his left big toe and shoulder ached. He'd been on his feet for hours and every joint in his body protested.

Apparently, waiting tables was for the younger crowd, but it was worth it.

Becca came behind the counter, poured a cup of coffee and set it down. "Here. You can at least have a cup before you leave. I guess you earned it."

"Thanks." He tried not to wince when he sat down, but his shoulder was on fire.

Becca set a bowl with little containers of creamer and a container of sugar packets in front of him. "You might want to ice that tonight. You're not used to carrying trays, clearing tables, or washing dishes. Your bursitis will act up for a couple of days."

"I didn't know you cared." He smiled.

"Don't try your lines on me," Becca huffed. "I'm not one of your little conquests that you can woo into believing anything that comes out of your mouth. You can't play me to get what you want."

Devon sat back, eyeing her for a moment. "What are you talking about?"

Becca popped one hip out to the side, resting her hand on it. "You always do this. You flirt and win over a girl then use her and toss her away."

"I didn't toss your mother away. She left," Devon said.

Becca pressed her lips together and raised both hands in surrender. "Whatever."

"No. Tell me what you want."

Becca eyed him suspiciously. "For you to leave town and never return. Don't try to contact me or follow me. I don't want to talk to you."

"Why? Rebecca, please. You need to tell me what I

did to make you so angry with me. I never cheated on your mother if that's what you think. I don't know what your mother told you, but I was faithful to her until the divorce papers came." Devon willed her to tell him something, anything. He needed to know what was wrong so he could fix it. There had to be a way to make things right. When he'd asked her back in New York if someone had hurt her, he thought the worst. That someone had attacked her or harmed her in some way, but she said it was him. That he'd done something, but she ran off without telling him what.

"You're a liar. You've lied to me my entire life. I don't believe anything you say anymore."

Each word she spoke slashed at his heart. "What? No. I never lied to you."

"See? I can't believe anything you say." Her eyes welled with tears.

He stood and opened his arms to pull her to him, to make all the pain go away and finally work things out, but she shuffled away and his arms dropped to his sides again. He knew if he pushed, she'd only run again. He wasn't sure why she hadn't run this time, why she hadn't taken off the moment she saw him walk into the coffee shop, but he was grateful. Perhaps she really did want to talk things out, but wasn't ready yet. He couldn't put his own needs before hers. He learned that when he'd dragged her home after the first time she'd run away. It had to be on her terms or it would never happen.

He decided to take the job at the community college and stick around. Perhaps someday, he'd return to Connecticut with her.

With a deep breath, he took money from his pants pocket and tossed a twenty on the counter. "You'll find a few checks behind the register and I placed the dirty dishes in that bin over there. Good night, Bec." He shuffled out of the diner and down the sidewalk. The night air had turned brisk, and his entire body complained. Not from the cold, but from his sorrow. His chest felt heavy, his lungs tight with emotion.

After a short walk, he found himself in front of the inn. The lights were off, indicating it was safe to return to his room without any unwelcomed interrogation. Not that he minded speaking with Mrs. Hatfield. It was just that he didn't want to talk to anyone right now.

The inn was silent, with only the faint sound of snoring from one of the guestrooms downstairs. He softly climbed the steps to his room, slipped off his shoes, pants, and shirt then collapsed into bed.

The digital clock on the nightstand became his nemesis as he watched it slowly climb through each hour until his eyes finally grew heavy around three in the morning. But sleep was fitful and short-lived. Around six, he got up, showered and dressed then walked downstairs in hopes of catching a glimpse of Becca going in for her morning shift at the coffee shop. Perhaps she'd be calmer today. He could order a coffee and sit and watch her work for a while without her running him out of the building.

He stood in his shadowy spot and waited for the café to open, but to his disappointment Mrs. Fletcher was the one to unlock the front door.

With a sigh, he stood there, wishing there was some way to bring a little happiness back into his life, or if not his then someone else's. Reading all those stories about Cathy Mitchell and hearing how she'd never been treated like the special person she was, he decided to do something nice to thank her for helping him. It had been a long time since he'd done anything genuine from the heart. The thought of opening himself up, even just in a friendly gesture made him uneasy. But it was time to start living again, to become a better man for Becca.

As he waited for the flower shop to open, he thought about different arrangements, but none of them were what he wanted. Then one thing came to mind.

"Can I help you?" the singsong voice of a young woman called as he walked into the shop.

"Yes. I'd like to order an orchid."

CHAPTER SEVEN

Cathy unlocked the front door of J & L Antiques and made her way to the back to place her stuff behind the counter. Her phone sang *My Boyfriend's Back*, and she slipped it from her pocket.

"Geesh, I haven't even opened to the public yet and you're already checking on me."

Judy chuckled. "Sorry. It's not that. I thought you might have questions and I was up early. It's not too easy to sleep when you're waiting to head to the hospital to find out if your granddaughter has cancer or not."

Cathy's chest tightened. She longed to give her friend a hug and make this all go away. "I'm so sorry. I wish there was something I could do."

"I know. If there was anything anyone could do, I know you'd make it happen."

A small glimmer of happiness filled her heart. "How's Lisa and Eric holding up?"

"Eric, and believe it or not, James are both taking it hard. This is the first baby James has ever held. I think this little girl represented so much to him, making up for the years he lost. He's putting on a brave face, of course, and tells me this isn't about him, but I know he's struggling." Her voice wavered. "Life can't be this cruel. Right when everything started going so well, how could it all fall apart? What if this causes a rift between Lisa and Eric? Or causes James to pull back into the world of hurt it took forty years for him to crawl out of?"

"Hush. Now you listen to me, Judy Benjamin. You are one of the strongest, most amazing women I know and you're not the type to play *what if* games. You straighten up and have faith, or I'm gonna be at that hospital by your side. And we both know you don't want that."

Judy chuckled. "Believe it or not, I do, but I need you there more. Lisa was concerned we'd lose a ton of business being closed this time of year. It's given her some peace knowing that you're handling the store." She sniffed then cleared her throat. "So, do you have any questions?"

"Nope. Don't worry. I've got this. You just concentrate on your family and don't worry about anything here. Got it?"

"Got it. Thank you," Judy whispered. "I'll call you later, after..."

Cathy's heart shrunk with despair, but she knew her friend needed her to remain strong. "You best call me with the good news. That's what best friends do. Got it?"

"Got it. Talk to you soon."

The line clicked off and Cathy sat down in a nearby chair, trying to make the spinning feeling stop. This couldn't be happening. Little Amelia was going to be okay. She just had to be. There was no way that baby girl had cancer. Lisa had been through enough with her ex and the loss of Amelia's twin. She couldn't lose Amelia, too.

The front door chimed and Cathy sat up. "Sorry. We're not open yet."

"I have a delivery for you, Cathy," Sherry called out. "And it looks like you could use something to brighten your day." She smiled.

How did an evil woman like Wonda give birth to such a sweet girl?

Sherry held up an orchid, beautifully delicate blooms of white with stains of purple hanging off the stem.

"Fate seems to be sending you a sign. I just received this by mistake yesterday. Then a handsome man came in and asked to purchase one for a special lady, but he didn't know where she lived. When he told me your name, I knew I had to get this to you as soon as possible."

Her sorrow faded and a hint of welcomed happiness surged through her. "That's for me?"

"Yes." Sherry walked through the shop, maneuvering around a bed and side table. "Here you go. Isn't it beautiful? The man didn't even ask how much it cost or anything. He just said whatever it took to get you an orchid. Said he never met a woman that deserved it more."

"Devon West." Her joy faded slightly.

Sherry set it down on the front desk. "Yeah. That's

him. He's gorgeous. Is he the man you met in the city? If so, I need to try internet dating."

She'd almost forgotten about her public humiliation with her internet date. With the memory, the pain in her hip returned and she rubbed it away.

"You don't look pleased. Don't you think it's pretty?"

Cathy stood up and eyed the gift. It looked amazing but promised nothing. "Yes, of course. It's lovely. Thank you so much for delivering it. And to answer your question, no. This isn't from the internet guy. That didn't go so well." She chuckled aloud. "I'd advise against the internet dating thing. It was a disaster for me, but if you ever decide to go for it, let me know. I'll have some words of wisdom for you."

"Thanks. I'm afraid the single men around here are few and far between." Sherry smiled then headed for the door. "I best get back. I have to finish the order for the Mason-Shaw wedding. Did you want to go through the details before I finished? Trianna said you might want final approval."

Cathy shook her head. "No. That's fine. She should do what she wants."

"Really?" Sherry's eyebrow rose. "You feeling okay?"

Cathy huffed. "Not you, too. You know I don't have to meddle in everyone's business. Only the ones who need it. Now, get going before I start looking for a date for you, too."

Sherry held up her hands in surrender. "I'm out of here."

The door chimed and she disappeared, leaving Cathy to stare at her orchid and wonder at the meaning behind it. Becca had warned her the man would make her feel special, and for a second she had. *Fool.* She had more important things to worry about than some man paying her false attention. She wasn't one of those pathetic lonely women who'd fall for his act. She'd read numerous reports about women who married the love of their life only to find out he was married to five other women in five different states. Yep, she was smarter than that.

Cathy sat the orchid at the end of the counter and flicked on the rest of the lights. She turned on soft music, dusted some furniture and straightened the knick-knacks clustered artfully on nearly every flat surface. If this was the only way she could help her friend, she'd do her best.

Within thirty minutes, the antique shop bustled with activity. People from several towns over had driven into Creekside just to shop for gifts at J & L Antiques. Lisa had proved herself a marketing genius with her Christmas specials and advertising in small town papers throughout the area.

"Can I help you with anything?" Cathy asked a woman a little younger than herself who had been eyeing an expensive vase. She looked tired, rough around the edges and more than a little jittery.

"That's okay. I'm just browsing right now," she answered with a forced smile. The woman scanned the shop nervously, making Cathy feel the need to keep a close eye out. She couldn't bear to mess up and let someone steal something from the shop. And since Judy knew every item in the store, she would know right away if something went missing.

"I'm ready to pay." Another woman smiled at Cathy and set her basket full of items on the counter.

Cathy walked around to the computer. In all the craziness, she'd never asked how to operate the darn thing. Being technically challenged, she didn't even have one at home. The clamminess of fear covered her skin as the blank screen mocked her. Forcing a smile, she placed her shaking fingers on the keyboard and started hitting keys, but nothing happened. The screen remained black. "Sorry. Just a second."

The woman eyed her suspiciously. "You might want to turn it on."

"Oh, silly me." Cathy waved her hand in front of her face. "Um...let me see."

The woman leaned over and pressed a button on the side of the big silver box beside the screen. "There you go. Do you have someone coming in soon to help you out? If so, I can browse some more on the street and come back later to pay for this."

"That would be great," Cathy said, relieved. "Thanks. I'll leave it right here. I'll have it all wrapped and ready to go when you return. Sound good?"

"Sounds perfect. I'll be back in about a half-hour."

Cathy glanced at the now illuminated screen. "Great."

The other patron continued to wonder around the store, but her eyes kept darting toward the front window. Cathy retrieved her cell phone and dialed

Rose. If anyone could help her with the computer, it was her former roommate and friend. Having graduated from high school, the young woman left for the university that summer. Cathy sighed. She missed Rose but knew the girl was happy and with the love of her life, Marcus Vega. Besides, they were better off in another city, away from her over-protective father and his prejudice against people from the other side of the creek.

The phone rang and rang. Finally, Cathy hung up and tried to think of who else might be able to help, but no one came to mind. She scanned the list of contacts Rose had set up in her phone before she left. Perhaps Karen Wanke, the secretary from church, could help. Or maybe Connie, Eric's secretary. They were both working ladies and probably knew how to use a computer.

The front door's bell chimed and Cathy looked up to see Devon standing there in black pants and a silver shirt that made his eyes and hair sparkle.

She shook her head. This man was bad news. Everything about him seemed contrived, as though he constantly had an end goal in mind.

"Good morning. I see you received my flower." He smiled, the kind men used when they thought they'd bribed their way out of the doghouse.

"Yes, I got it." Cathy watched the woman duck behind a large folding screen and headed that way to intercept her.

"Hey, I thought you liked orchids. Did I remember wrong?" he asked.

"No. It's not that." As Cathy got closer, the woman shot out the front door. She sighed. "I thought that woman might be shoplifting."

"That's not good. Want me to go after her?"

She shook her head. "No. It's okay. I don't think she made it out with anything. What are you doing here anyway?" Cathy rubbed the back of her neck and leaned against the counter.

Devon closed the distance between them. "You don't seem happy to see me."

She eyed the orchid. "You don't need to bribe me. If I decide to help you with your daughter, I'll help."

Devon's brows knitted together. "Are you always so suspicious?"

She straightened her scarf, keeping her eyes on her hands. "Only with men who like to smooth-talk women."

"Ouch," Devon said. "I promise you I sent you the orchid for no other reason than I wanted to see you smile. It was a friendly gesture. No attachments."

Cathy studied him, trying to decide if his words were sincere or full of crap like Becca had warned.

The door chimed again and four ladies came inside. Cathy bit her bottom lip absently. One of them had to be Wonda. *Ugh, she probably came just to see me fall flat on my face.* That woman was a thorn in her side.

"Do you need some help?" Devon leaned toward her, resting his elbow on the counter. His cologne drew her closer, promising an adventure with its spicy and exotic scent.

She shook her head and rounded the corner, eyeing her two nemeses, the computer and Wonda.

"What's wrong?"

What's wrong? Everything.

"I'm supposed to be working the store for my best friend who's at the hospital right now waiting to find out if her grandbaby has cancer, but I don't know how to use one of those things." She jerked her head toward the computer.

"You mean the computer?" Devon smiled and squeezed her shoulder. "Now, that's something I can help with. I'm done with manual labor and would welcome sitting at a computer all day. My feet still hurt from yesterday."

What exactly has he been doing? she wondered. "You like those things? They give me a headache."

Devon rounded the counter and covered the mouse thingy with his hand, clicking a few things. "You know her password?"

"Yes."

He stood back and turned to the side. "Go ahead and enter it. I promise not to look." He winked.

She pecked out *Truelove40* as quickly as she could then scooted out of his way.

"Okay, let's see what we've got here." His fingers flew across the keys. "Is this an order that needs to be rung up," he asked, pointing to the basket of items on the counter. At her nod, he lifted a scented candle from the basket, pressed a few keys, entered some information then set it down to grab the next item.

A woman with dark glasses and a long thin nose

set down a beautiful Christmas ornament.

"You all set?" he asked as he lifted it and copied some numbers into the computer. Then he looked up. "That will be thirty-two-seventy, with tax. Will you be paying by cash, check, or credit card?"

"Credit," she smiled, handing him a card.

"Great." He ran the card through a slotted device beside the keyboard and a receipt printed. Cathy had barely managed to wrap the item and tuck it into a bag in the amount of time it took him to complete the transaction. "Thank you so much for shopping with us today," he said as he took the bag from Cathy, slipping the receipt inside before handing it over to the woman.

"My pleasure," she giggled.

The man was beyond charming. It infuriated Cathy to see the woman practically fall at his feet. *Just like Becca had said.*

The woman returned to her friends, the bunch of them acting like cackling hens in heat.

Then Wonda sauntered over. "So, who do we have here?"

Cathy fisted her hands at her sides. "Did you want to purchase something or are you just going to browse like usual?"

Wonda flicked her cashmere scarf around her neck. "I'm not the one who's broke, dear."

Cathy narrowed her gaze. How'd that woman know she had financial issues?

Devon shot his hand out. "I'm Devon West."

"What are you doing back there, Devon?" Wonda leaned against the counter, fluttering her fake lashes at him.

The hussie.

"I'm enjoying a day with the most beautiful lady in Creekside." Devon reached out and placed a strong arm around Cathy's shoulder, pulling her into his side. He'd already won her over, helping her conquer her technical nemesis. But now, she wanted to lay a big kiss on him when Wonda's mouth dropped faster than her breasts without her push-up bra.

"Well, it was a pleasure to meet you. We're headed to Café Bliss if you'd care for a cup." Wonda waved behind her as she rejoined her entourage.

Cathy stiffened.

"I appreciate the offer, but I'm happy here." Devon squeezed Cathy tighter to his side and kissed the side of her head.

Take that, Cathy thought as she watched Wonda's retreating back.

The door chimed and Devon slipped away. "I know I promised to behave myself, but I didn't like the way that woman was behaving. I promise to keep my hands to myself from now on."

"No. It's fine," Cathy mumbled.

"In that case..." He slipped his arm back around Cathy and she rolled her eyes.

"You just had to ruin it, didn't you?" She playfully shoved him away.

Devon winked at her then turned his attention back to the computer. "Do you want me to show you how to run this, or should I stick around and help? I don't mind staying if you'd like. I don't have any plans this afternoon anyway."

She wanted to tell him to take a hike, but even her pride didn't mean as much as not failing Judy when she needed her most. Besides, anyone that could make Wonda leave with her tail between her legs was all right in Cathy's book. "I guess you can stay," she shrugged, straightening a crystal swan on a glass stand.

"So, you want me to stay?" Devon nudged.

She turned to tell him to get over himself, but the door opened again and a gaggle of tourists entered. With a sigh, she admitted defeat. "Yes. I want you to stay."

Devon's mouth curled into a triumphant smile. "I'll go see if I can help them then."

"I'll go. You stay behind that silver box from Hell."

Devon laughed aloud, the baritone sound mingling with the Christmas music softly crooning from the speakers above.

Cathy marched to the Christmas decoration section and plastered on a fake smile. "Hi there. How can I help you today?"

"Oh, my friend bought a darling Christmas star here. It's so lovely. Do you have another one?" asked a woman in a bright red sweater.

Cathy thought back and remembered Judy mentioning most of the ornaments were handmade and one of a kind. "I'm afraid not. Each ornament is unique."

"Can I order one to be made? I need a gift for an impossible to please mother-in-law. And an ornament like that would be perfect."

"Let me check behind the desk and see if I can locate the artist's information." Cathy trotted behind the counter and whispered to Devon, "Can you see if Judy has any information in there on an artist that makes ornaments?"

"I can try. Let's take a look in the folders."

Cathy glanced below the counter. "I don't see any folders. She does everything on that darn silver box."

Devon laughed again. "I didn't mean those types of folders."

Cathy huffed. "Well, how should I know?"

He placed a hand on the small of her back. "You really don't know much about computers, do you?"

Cathy knew she should scoot away. His touch and the trail of warmth it left behind would only play with her emotions. But she leaned into his side instead, eyeing the computer screen. "I didn't even know how to turn it on."

"I guess I should give you some lessons." He returned his fingers to the keyboard. "Ah, here we go. I think I found the right folder."

The printer sounded and Cathy retrieved the paper. "Thanks."

"You're welcome." He walked over to where a couple was perusing some furniture and handled them like a pro.

Was he really a salesman, not a college professor? How could she trust anything he said?

Cathy shoved the thought from her head and read down the sheet in her hand. *Special orders upon request. Two weeks turnaround or a ten percent charge for expediting.*

Walking back over to the woman in the red sweater, she said, "Ma'am, it looks like he can do special orders, but there'll be an upcharge for getting it by Christmas."

The lady looked over the top of her glasses at Cathy. "How much?"

"Ten percent."

"That's fine. I'll go ahead and place the order." She followed Cathy to the counter then waited as Cathy wrote down all the specifics, hoping she didn't forget to ask anything important.

"I'll call you as soon as it arrives. How would you like to pay?"

"Credit, please." The woman removed her wallet and handed her the card. Cathy eyed the machine with trepidation. She'd watched how he'd run the card last time, but wasn't sure she would get it right. *Screw it. I'm a smart lady. I'll manage.* She put her hand on the mouse thingy, but nothing happened. The screen remained dark. "Goodness gracious."

"Something wrong?"

"Sorry, ma'am. I don't run the computer. Let me get Devon for you."

The woman huffed. "I don't have time for this." She turned and spotted Devon sauntering up to the counter. "Oh, I guess I could spare a few minutes."

Cathy didn't like the way the woman looked at him, like a cougar eyeing fresh meat in a desert. When he came behind the counter, she slid her hand into the crook of his arm. She couldn't help herself. "I appreciate your help," she crooned. "Oh, and the flower. It really was beautiful." She glanced at the woman, who now glowered at her, before walking over to tell a small child to stop touching the crystal swans. When she returned, he crossed his arms over his chest and leaned back against the wall with a smug smile.

"What?"

"So, you did like my flower." He winked.

"It's pretty. Don't make too much of it," she snipped.

The woman with the child left, leaving the shop empty save for a couple browsing behind the large folding screen.

He approached her, pinning her back to the counter. "Why did you decide at that moment to tell me you liked the flower?" He placed a hand on either side of her and lowered his head to meet her gaze, his face only inches from hers.

She couldn't think with that womanizing cologne distracting her. "Don't make more out of it than you should."

"I don't think I'm making too much out of it." He lowered his head further, his cheek brushing her skin, and she thought she'd lose consciousness. A warm breath caressed her ear and she grasped the counter behind her to remain upright. "I think you were jealous," he whispered.

She swallowed so loud she was sure he could hear it, and based on his grin, he had. The tantalizing cologne, softly sparkling lights, quiet music... The earth spun beneath her and she feared it would never be steady again. His deep, dark eyes sucked her in and for a moment, she was lost.

The front door chimed, breaking the spell, and she ducked under his arm. "Good morning. Welcome to J & L Antiques." She spoke as cheerfully as possible, but the rasp in her voice confessed he'd managed to break the barrier of rationality.

"Yes, I'm looking for a Jesus figurine to complete my POC nativity scene," said a lady with a scar down her cheek.

"Certainly. Let's take a look over here." Cathy held out a hand to direct the soft-spoken woman to the back of the store. The scar on her face drew her attention, but Cathy quickly averted her gaze.

"It's okay."

"What's okay?" Cathy asked.

"You can look at my scar. I'm proud of it," the woman said, smiling with enthusiasm. "I'm Grace. I just returned home after a second tour in Afghanistan. This scar reminds me I survived."

Cathy clutched her chest. "Oh, darling. It's amazing to meet such a brave person who can still smile."

"Thank you. Everyday that I can look at my daughter, or hug my husband is a miracle. This will be our first Christmas since I returned and I want to make it special. My little girl's learning about Jesus in Bible study and is upset that I only have John, Mary, a donkey, sheep, and the manger right now. My husband always bought me a piece for my collection every Christmas, but I'm afraid we can't find Jesus from the

Passion of Christ collection anywhere."

"Well, let's see what we have." Cathy searched the table displaying nativity figurines and the two shelves behind it, with no sign of baby Jesus, but she refused to give up. With one hand on the table, she lowered to the ground and pulled out a few boxes marked POC figurines.

"Can I help you with something?" Devon asked behind her.

She froze, suddenly realizing she was on her hands and knees with her butt sticking out for all to see. The sweater she wore over the leggings was flattering when standing, but skin tight when she bent over. She scurried out from underneath the table, hitting her head and knocking several things over with a loud *clang*.

Devon kneeled by her side and placed a hand on her head to guide her out from under the table. "Are you okay?"

Mortified, Cathy wanted to crawl back under it, but if Grace could walk around proud of her scar, Cathy could handle a few snickers. "I'm fine. Just old and klutzy."

"I find you to be neither." His hand covered hers, and instead of finding mirth in his expression, she saw concern. "You sure you're okay?"

"Yes. Only damaged my pride." She chuckled and sat back on her boots. "Let's check these three boxes and see what we have. If we don't find it, then you can leave your name and number and when the owner calls, I'll ask her where we can get one."

"I'm afraid it won't be that easy. I've already searched all the websites and auctions and such. It's nowhere to be found." The joy in her voice faded. "I know it should be enough that I'm home, but I just wanted to give my little girl a special present for being so brave while I was away."

Devon opened a box. "Then we'll just have to find one for you. I have a little girl of my own and I'd move Heaven and Earth to give her what she wanted or needed in life. Every child is a blessing."

Cathy glanced up at the man by her side, the same one Becca had made out to be a horrible womanizer, cheater and bad father. This didn't sound like the man she'd described. He sounded more like a loving father. Was he playing Cathy even now, or had Becca lied?

Cathy opened the next box, swatting away the dust that tickled her nose. Several figurines were wrapped and firmly packed inside. She unwrapped the first few and set them neatly on the tabletop. One after another, she found various decorative figures, but none of them were baby Jesus. When the final figurine rested on the table, they all looked at one another in dismay.

"This doesn't mean J & L Antiques doesn't have it, or can't get it," Cathy declared. "Judy's a wiz at finding items for people. Let's take down your name and number just in case, and we'll do all we can to get that Jesus figurine to you by Christmas."

Grace clapped her hands together. "That would be amazing. Thank you so much! Any help would be greatly appreciated, but I doubt you can get it that quickly."

Cathy's phone sang *My Boyfriend's Back.* "Devon? Do you mind taking down her information? I have to get this."

"Certainly." He led Grace to the counter and entered her personal information into the computer while Cathy dashed to the phone.

"Hello? Judy?"

Only a muffled sob answered.

"Judy? Are you there?"

"Yes, I'm here."

At Judy's whimpered tone, Cathy wanted to reach through the phone and pull her friend into her arms. She took a long breath then asked, "What is it?"

For a long moment only the sound of doctors being paged, elevators beeping and Judy's shuddering breath came over the line. Cathy gripped the side of the counter.

"It's cancer...probably Leukemia."

CHAPTER EIGHT

Devon and Grace stood at the counter, watching the color drain from Cathy's face. What had happened?

"I'm so sorry," she whispered into the phone.

A jolt of concern bolted through him and he willed the news to not be horrible. He'd been through enough of that the last year. He didn't wish that on anyone, especially the woman that had obviously brought so much comfort to others.

He turned to Grace. "I'll call as soon as we know anything. I can assure you that if anyone will make it happen, it's that woman over there. She's single-handedly taken down an assassin who tried to kill her friend. She practically runs this town and loves everyone in it."

"It's so nice to see a couple that's been together so long still look at each other with that passion and fire in their eyes. You two are an inspiration." Grace beamed at him.

"Oh, we're...thank you." He didn't know why he didn't correct her. Perhaps because, for a second, it felt good for someone to think he was life partners with such an amazing woman, someone that would brave the hardships in life without withering. "Have a good day."

Grace nodded then shot a sideways glance at Cathy. "I hope everything's okay."

"Me, too." Devon watched the woman exit then turned to Cathy. At the sight of her wavering on her feet, he grabbed a chair and guided her down to sit.

"Call me later when you know more." Cathy ended the call and her hands collapsed onto her lap, the phone limp in her fingers.

Devon knelt in front of her, lowering to her eye level. "Are you okay?"

Cathy rotated her head to the left then the right, her eyes distant.

He stroked her arm. "What can I do?"

"I wish I knew. I feel so helpless." Cathy stroked the phone with her thumb. "I want to be there, but it's better for her if I'm here. But it's hard to stay behind when your best friend is falling apart."

"Where is she? Why can't you go to her?" Devon asked.

"It's not that. I could drive the few hours to the hospital. It's just, she has her family there and it's best I stay here and keep an eye on the store. But I'm not good at feeling useless. I need to do something, but I don't know what."

He took her hands in his and held them tight. "I'm here for you. Anything you need, you just let me know."

Finally, she met his gaze. "I think I need a hug," she whispered.

"It would be my pleasure." He guided her up from the seat then wrapped his arms around her. Holding her tight against him, he stroked her hair. It smelled like fresh lilac in an open field. Her heart beat against his chest and her cheek rested on his shoulder. He'd had women in his arms plenty of time in the last few years, but never felt such intimacy. It was...nice, nicer than any other conjugal acts he had with others. Yet, he couldn't explain this deep connection. The feeling he could only imagine Grace felt when she hugged her husband for the first time after coming home from war. A meaningful embrace, full of hope and promise.

"That computer thing. Can you help me with a little research?"

He leaned back, and she lifted her head. Her pink cheeks remained dry, but he yearned to touch them, to see if they were as soft as they looked. They were. "Sure, I'd be happy to help." But he didn't want to let her go. He could stand there with her in his arms for the rest of the day and still not have enough. "What do you want to research?"

Cathy straightened and lifted her head. It was the look she had in the picture he saw online when she'd plowed her car into the SUV to save her friend. Her jaw was set with a strength he'd never seen in any woman. "I want to know about juvenile Leukemia and the ways to treat it. What kind of things help? What is the prognosis?"

Devon traced a fine line from the edge of her eye to her temple, memorizing its shape and texture. "I can help with that." Still not wanting to release her, he took her hand and sat her down on the bar stool at the counter. Then he stood behind her and reached an arm out on each side of her to reach the keyboard. The sound of a quick inhale caught his attention, but he didn't say anything. He only smiled at the encouragement. "Let's see." He typed *Leukemia in children* into the search engine. Pages of results appeared, with links to websites full of information.

For hours, they clicked, browsed, and read then moved on to another site between helping the customers that wandered into the shop. The sky darkened outside, as if reflecting the ominous mood in the room. By mid–afternoon, snowflakes began to fall.

"It looks like we're going to get some snow," Devon said.

Cathy shook her head. "It's too early. We usually don't get snow until January or February around here."

"Well, you might want to tell the weather that. It looks like icy rain, actually." He brought up another browser to check the weather report and read through the warnings for icy rain in the area. "Yep, looks like a storm's coming. Do you want me to drive you home?"

Cathy chuckled. "It'll take more than a few inches of sleet to worry me. I'll be fine. Here, check this link." She pointed a red-painted nail at the screen. He clicked and it pulled up the list of treatments for Leukemia. Chemotherapy, bone marrow transplants, and operations were listed, just as they'd been on many other sites. But this one showed the list of complications with each treatment. Not just the physical complications, but the financial as well.

Bone marrow transplant seemed like the best option but it also added an additional concern. *Lack of bone marrow donors and the difficulty of finding a match means this treatment isn't feasible for many patients,* he read. *In most cases, parents are not viable donors.*

Cathy shot up. "That's it. I'll organize a way to help them with treatment. Financially and finding donors. Anything they need, we'll be ready. And I know just who to get to help me." Without missing a beat, she snatched her phone and started scrolling through her contacts.

The woman he already suspected to be an integral member of the community, always willing to put others before herself, demonstrated just how deep her determination went.

"That'll be a lot of work. And there's no guarantees."

"Doesn't matter. If there's even the slightest chance it will help, I'll do it. This is what I do. I fix things. It gives me purpose in life." Cathy hopped off the stool. "You think you can watch things around here for a bit? I need to run an errand."

"Sure," Devon shrugged, "but it'll cost you dinner. Well, your company at dinner. I'll buy."

Cathy shook her head. "You never give up, do you?"

"Not when the woman is worth the attention."

Cathy rolled her eyes. "Okay, fine. Only because you helped me out today. Don't think I'm falling for your charms, though, because I ain't."

Devon held up his hands. "I wouldn't dream that such a sophisticated, attractive, and obviously determined woman would fall for any such nonsense." He smiled. "Trust me. I'll behave."

Cathy snagged her purse and headed for the door. "Fine. A girl's got to eat anyway."

Devon remained standing behind the counter long after she'd disappeared. For the first time in ages, he felt like he had something worth while to focus on, besides his loneliness.

He went over to the figurines they'd unpacked and repacked them, tucking them back under the table where Cathy had found them. Then he updated the computer software on the machine, changed a few light bulbs that had gone out and even straightened the stacks of papers behind the desk. But still Cathy hadn't returned.

Idle time was his enemy, allowing his thoughts to waver to his past and his choices. He'd let Becca run him out of New York, but not this time. After helping his best friend bury his twenty-one-year-old son, who'd died in a car accident, Devon knew he couldn't leave without setting things right with his daughter. That was why he'd sold his house, quit his job and came to Creekside.

Had he lost his mind? Was all of this for nothing?

Images of his best friend, a broken man at his son's funeral, stung Devon's heart. If that had been Becca... He didn't even want to think about it, but there was always *what ifs*. What if something happened to her, or him, and he never got the chance to see things through? What if she spent the rest of her life hating him for something he didn't even know he did? He knew he had to force her to tell him what happened, and this time he wasn't going to let her out of it. His life had no meaning without her in it, and it was time to take action.

The wall clock chimed the hour. With the store empty of customers, he kept busy by searching for the baby Jesus figurine on wholesale, auction, and trading websites, but he quickly discovered it was a much sought-after item this time of year.

Perhaps if he'd taken his family to church more they would have found the bond that people claim to have. The kind that keeps families together, no matter what happened.

Defeated, he abandoned his search and went to straighten the bedding and candles the little boy had played with earlier then picked up the candy wrappers he'd left behind. Standing, he caught a glimpse of a woman in a white coat with jet-black hair. He froze. *It couldn't be.* He had to be imagining things.

The wrappers slipped from his fingers as he rushed to open the front door. A chill swept through his soul. "Kimmie?"

The woman passed a couple strolling along the sidewalk then crossed the street beyond his line of sight toward the coffee shop.

"No, she can't be."

He darted out the door. Running, he weaved through the few people remaining on the street until he reached the end of the building. A grayness shadowed the walkway, but there was no sign of the woman. Was he losing his mind? Seeing things that weren't there?

He shook it off and after one more glance, trotted back to the antique store. The road was empty, not a soul out braving the freezing rain that came down harder now. Everyone had no doubt taken refuge in the diner or coffee shop. Yet, the hair on the back of his neck stood at attention. He couldn't ignore the feeling that someone was watching him. With one more sideways glance, he returned to the warm, inviting interior of the shop.

Pulling his cell phone from his pocket, he dialed the investigator again. This time, the man answered.

"Harper P.I."

"Hey, Harper. It's West. I wanted to know if you located my ex-wife yet."

"Hi, Mr. West," Harper said cheerfully. Then he sighed. "Not exactly, but I've narrowed down the area she seems to be frequenting right now." He cleared his throat and papers shuffled in the background. "It appears she's somewhere in the southeast. Tennessee, to be specific."

"Did you say Tennessee?" Devon fell onto the stool behind him. *Was that really her?*

"Yes, that's right. I should have where she's staying after I dig a little deeper. But I'm not even sure of the last name she's using right now. She was released from a women's correctional facility two months ago, after being incarcerated for fraud and tax evasion. Apparently, she'd been claiming dependents on her income tax forms and some other various crimes. One man even proved she'd married him then stole tens of thousands of dollars from his bank account before running off. She was released early on good behavior and prison overcrowding." Harper sighed again. "Unfortunately, she's not using any credit cards under her maiden or married name. But something popped for a card issued under a fake name. She must've still had some money tied up with that name from before she was incarcerated. She used it to buy some clothes and rent a car. It popped again for a gas station in Tennessee. I'm not sure where she's headed, but I know how to track her now, so it won't be long."

Prison? Fraud? Had everything she'd ever told him been a lie. She'd spent half their savings then she told him she never loved him and left, but he didn't know she could resort to criminal activity. He shouldn't have been surprised, though.

"If she's really in Tennessee, that makes me nervous. That's where my daughter is right now. Please let me know the second you find anything else about her location."

"I will."

Devon eyed the box of figurines under the table. "Oh, and I have one more job for you, but it isn't the usual detective work."

"I've heard it all," Harper laughed. "And you pay well, so shoot and I'll let you know what I can do."

"I want you to find a baby Jesus POC, uh, that stands for Passion of Christ, figurine and have it delivered to Creekside in care of J & L Antiques. I warn you, it's like the Tickle Me Elmo craze of 1996. It's a

99

ghost item and probably impossible to find."

"Nothing is impossible. I'll get on it."

The phone clicked off. Devon clutched it, praying his ex-wife wasn't headed for this town. If so, she could ruin any happiness Becca might have found in the last two years. Not to mention his chance of finding out what happened before she ran off again.

He stood and crossed the room to the front windows. Ice began to build on the sidewalks outside. He hoped his daughter didn't have far to walk or drive. He'd go check on her when they closed up shop, even if it was only to watch from a distance.

The clock chimed again. *Where in the world is Cathy?* It had been two hours since she left, and with the treacherous conditions outside, he worried for her safe return. After another hour, he gave up waiting and decided to try calling her. He searched his phone log for her number and dialed, but her voicemail immediately picked up.

Before he could leave a message, the door chimed and he looked up. "Welcome—"

His blood ran cold. Beyond the customer that had just walked in, he caught a glimpse of a woman walking along the opposite side of the street. With black hair, a petite frame, and a swagger that would turn a man's head, he knew without a doubt who she was.

Kimmie.

CHAPTER NINE

Cathy arrived at Karen Wanke's house to the sound of a yapping dog and ice forming on the front steps. With one hand on the white wooden railing, leading to the Cape Cod style house, she carefully climbed up to the periwinkle front door.

"Willy! Down, boy." Karen opened the door and a hyperactive Russell Terrier with brown ears and gray spots ran out to sniff Cathy's boots.

"His name's Willy?" Cathy asked. "Willy Wanke? As in Willy Wonka and the Chocolate Factory?"

"Yep." Karen lifted the small dog and tucked him into her side, probably so she didn't get dog hair on her *Cupcake Lady* apron. "Come on in."

Cathy hadn't been inside Karen's home in years. Yet it hadn't changed much with its eclectic style. It was adorable and felt lived-in. "Thank you so much for meeting with me."

"No worries, but as I said, I'll need to chat in the kitchen. I'm working." She set Willy on the floor then patted toward the kitchen at the back of the house.

The smell of fresh vanilla, hazelnut, chocolate, and everything else yummy swirled to her nose, testing her willpower. "They all smell so delicious. Who are these for?"

"They're for the seniors. I promised Trianna I'd drop them by the recreation center around noon tomorrow when they have their bingo tournament."

"Not right now, but that's awful nice of you. Do they pay you for that?"

Karen shook her head and pressed her glasses up the bridge of her nose. "Oh, these few won't matter in the grand scheme of things. Besides, I like to visit with Frank and the rest of the old dogs." She chuckled. "That's what they've branded themselves. It's also a tasting for Trianna and Sheriff Mason since I'll be handling their wedding in a few days."

Cathy thought back to the conversations she'd had with the couple over their wedding plans and didn't recall approving cupcakes. She opened her mouth to protest, but noticed a cupcake with perfect white frosting and beading on top, next to a chocolate one with a tuxedo strawberry. It looked adorable. Besides, she had too many other things to worry about right now. "I think that's lovely."

Karen picked up a piping bag and started squeezing frosting that appeared to have crushed Oreos in it onto a cupcake. "Really? You're not going to tell me how it's a huge mistake for them to serve cupcakes at their wedding? Are you feeling okay?"

"Don't be silly." Cathy waved at her dismissively. "Listen, I need to ask you for a favor."

Karen set the bag on the counter and sprinkled more crushed cookies on top. "Sure. Shoot."

"Well, since you work as secretary at the church, I thought you'd be able to help me organize a fundraiser and bone marrow matching program." At Karen's stunned look, she hurried to continue. "You see, little Amelia is sick. She has Leukemia. I read up on it and it looks like she might have to do chemo and a bone marrow transplant."

Karen rested her hands against the counter and leaned over. "I'm so sorry. That's horrible news, but isn't Amelia too young for a bone marrow transplant?"

"No. It's hard to find a donor, though. The best match is usually a sibling, but that might be hard to locate. I'm going to try to contact that awful Mark from New York to see if I can find any of his offspring, but I doubt he'll cooperate."

"Based on his behavior when Lisa was in the hospital, I'd say that'll be an impossible task. Besides, didn't he want her to get an abortion?"

Cathy nodded. "Yeah. He made it clear he didn't want kids, but even if there's a slim chance, I've got to try. That's why I need your help with a fundraiser I want to hold during the Final Day of Shopping event on December 23rd. Everyone from several towns over will be here. I'm also going to call the girls from the Red Hat Society, my friend at the mayor's office, and see if Sheriff Mason can get the police, fire and rescue to help. You know everyone loves Judy Benjamin. I'm sure the entire town will pull together if they know what's going on."

Karen cocked an eyebrow. "Does Judy know you're going to tell the entire town about Amelia? Do Lisa and

Eric know?"

Cathy huffed. "This is about saving a little girl's life."

Karen sighed, moved around the kitchen island to stand next to Cathy, and placed a hand on her shoulder. "You sure you're not trying to save the day to make up for all those years you kept that secret from Judy about James being alive?"

Cathy stepped back and narrowed her gaze. "Don't be silly. That's water under the bridge."

The oven beeped, drawing Karen's attention. "I can set up something at the church and circulate an email chain. There has to be a match somewhere in this town, but we'll get the word out to all of Tennessee just in case. Besides, treatment can be expensive and they'll need all the help they can get. I'm pretty sure we can raise some good money for Amelia."

"I think so, too." Cathy smiled then glanced longingly at the cupcake. "Hey, does your offer for a cupcake still stand?"

"Sure. I was afraid I was losing my touch. You're looking awful skinny these days, though."

"It's not for me. Devon's watching the shop and I thought I'd take him a cupcake as a *thank you.*"

Karen took out a small cardboard box and folded it into a square. "Who's Devon? I don't recall anyone by that name being in town."

"He's new here. I just thought I should give him something as *thanks* for helping out while I came here to talk to you."

Karen gestured to the completed cupcakes on the

counter and Cathy pointed to the cookie one she'd been working on.

"Based on that look on your face, this Devon's a lucky man."

"What?" Cathy slapped her hand to her chest. "Don't be absurd."

Karen handed her the box, the cupcake tucked safely inside. "If you say so."

Cathy huffed then turned on her heel. "Let me know when you send the email and I'll do research on how to do the bone marrow matching."

"Sounds good. Maybe I'll stop by and meet this Devon tomorrow on my way to the rec center. My husband's still up in Canada for work, so I have plenty of time. I'd like to meet our newcomer and see what's got Cathy Mitchell in such a state." She smirked as she ushered Cathy out the door while keeping one foot in front of Willy. "Talk to you tomorrow." She shut the door before Cathy could object.

"How rude," Cathy muttered as she made her way down the damp street. Luckily, the ice hadn't gotten any worse. It had taken her awhile to go home, make her calls then get to Karen's. The sky was darker now. She glanced down at her watch, shocked to find she'd been gone for three hours.

She hopped into Judy's car and barreled down the street back toward Main. The crowds had all but disappeared from town, and with the icy weather, they likely wouldn't be back. She'd go ahead and close up shop then head to dinner with Devon. He'd been so kind all day. The least she could do was oblige him.

A part of her wanted to believe that Becca was just a problem child who'd run away from home without just cause. But she didn't know either of them well enough yet to decide who was lying and who was telling the truth. Perhaps the entire thing was a misunderstanding. If so, she'd do what she could to bring those two back together.

Devon certainly had his moments, but when he let go of his arrogant player persona, she found him sweet, sincere, and handsome. The orchid he'd bought for her was exquisite, and how many men would remember it was her favorite flower, or pay that much for it?

She cringed at the thought of how much it must have cost. In her financial situation, it would have been better for him to pay the property taxes on her house than given her a flower. But for once, frugality didn't win out and her heart warmed at the thought of the gesture. Perhaps she'd judged him too harshly. After all, her late husband had never bought her flowers. Of course, he'd invested all their money in high risk stocks and lost almost all of it before his death, leaving her with little income. She'd hated him for it for a while, then she let the anger go and realized they'd had a good life. He'd provided for her until the end. Perhaps if he was still alive they could've worked out their money problems somehow.

As desperate as she was, she couldn't bear to tell anyone. It was too embarrassing. Her and her husband had always been well off and she couldn't stand to face the pitying gazes when folks discovered her house was on the market for owing back taxes on the property.

The thought of losing her home made her sad, but she reminded herself that things could be worse and concentrated on something she could control.

Amelia would get that transplant and they'd raise enough money to ease the financial burden Lisa and Eric would soon be faced with. But first, she wanted to give Devon his cupcake. It wasn't much, but it was her own way of telling him she'd stop judging him so harshly and give him a chance.

Sheriff Mason drove down Main Street toward her and rolled to a stop, his hand rotating to indicate she should open her window.

She stopped beside his car and put her window down. "What's going on, sheriff?"

"Just wanted to tell you to get off the road. The county doesn't have salt or sand yet, so the icy conditions are going to be a problem. You'll need to park your car here and walk. There's black ice at the end of the street. I was just about to rope it off."

"I need to get back to J & L Antiques first," Cathy said, pointing in the direction of the shop.

"I've already told all the shop owners, diner and coffee house to shut down until the sun's up in the morning. School's been canceled for tomorrow, too. More rain is heading this way and with this temperature it won't take long for the roads to be a mess."

"Understood. I'll just lock up and head home. Good luck tonight. If you get stuck out here or need something, my door's always open."

"Thanks, Cathy. I appreciate that. You've always

been my number one deputy." He smiled before pulling away.

Cathy liked that man. He was honest and hardworking. It broke her heart when his first wife left him. But Trianna would make a great wife. A challenge for sure, but a great wife.

With the town deserted, she had her pick of parking spaces. Getting out of the car, she spotted the front door to the antique shop ajar. Her heart stuttered at the sight. With a tentative step, she snuck up to the side of the building and peeked through the window.

Devon sat with his head in his hands at the table. She rushed inside, with her pepper spray key chain in hand, and glanced around. "Everything okay in here?"

Devon lifted his head, a look of desperation on his face. "I'm going to lose her. Again."

CHAPTER TEN

Devon's gut clenched tight and he thought the world would spin out of control once more. The nightmare his wife had created five years ago was about to repeat itself and there was nothing he could do about it. He'd thought it would be good to know where Kimmie was, to finally get some closure and share the information with Becca if she ever asked. He had hoped knowing would be a way for them to grieve together. But now that she was in the same zip code as his fragile daughter, he couldn't help worrying.

"Who?" Cathy whispered before pulling a chair up next to him and taking his hands in hers.

"My daughter, Becca." He squeezed her hand tight. "You don't understand. Her mother's crazy. She walked out on us without a word then sent divorce papers a few years later. It wasn't until today I found out she married another man. Apparently, she'd married him for money. Kimmie always loved money, had to have the best of everything. Her husband pressed charges when she ran off with a small fortune. She served time for it, too, and for fraud, theft and a bunch of other things. She just got out of prison."

Cathy rubbed her thumb over his hand and it soothed him in a way he hadn't felt since childhood. The world seemed a little less bleak with her by his side.

"I'm so sorry. Did she try to contact you? Is that why you're upset and worried about Becca?"

He took in a long breath. "She's here, in town. I don't know why, but she must have been trying to track down Becca."

A car drove past slowly, drawing their attention. Christmas music still played quietly overhead, helping to calm his soul a bit.

He took a deep breath. "I can't let Kimmie talk to Becca. She caused my daughter to suffer some sort of psychotic break when she left. Becca ran away from home when she was just thirteen. The second time, it took me months to track her down in New York City. She convinced the people around her that I was this horrible man, and when she refused to come home, I left." He lowered his head in shame. "I left my daughter in a city where she only had some new friends. No family or loved ones to protect her. She had so much hatred for me, I didn't know what to do. Since she was eighteen, I couldn't force her to go home. She'd been out of control since she was sixteen, getting into trouble with boys and alcohol. But she was smart and had great grades. I just...don't know what happened. She still won't talk to me."

Cathy cleared her throat. "I hope you don't mind me asking, but if you left her in New York, why did you follow her here?"

"Because. I'd watched a friend bury his son and I couldn't go through that. I had to find my Becca again, make sure she was safe and happy. No matter what, we have to talk. Even if she hates me, I need to know why so I can try to make amends. And I need her to know that I love her with all my heart. If she thought I had replaced her with other women, I need her to know that could never happen. I tried to deal with my grief in my own way, shielding my heart from any woman that came into my life. But it wasn't right for her or for me. I was never that guy, even when I acted like it. Now, my daughter's going to come face to face with a woman who abandoned her and I'm not by her side." He bolted from his seat. "I need to find her. I'll go to the diner and the coffee house. I'll make her listen to me."

Cathy rubbed his shoulder. "She's not there."

"What do you mean?" he asked as he marched to the door.

"The town's shut down for the night. Sheriff's roping off the roads. There's no way to get to her since she's outside of town, which means your ex can't either." Cathy walked up behind him and placed a hand on either side of his waist. He took them and wrapped them around his body. She rested her cheek to his back and for a moment, he relaxed.

"What happened?" he asked, remembering her errand. "Did you work something out for Amelia?" The heat of her arms reminded him of what it was like to actually have someone to care about, to not be alone all the time.

"Yes. We worked out a plan to help. I'll be talking

to Karen about it some more tomorrow."

He turned in her arms and pulled her close. Looking down into her soft eyes, he thought he could forget all his troubles for a few minutes and just be with her. "I promised you dinner."

"I'm afraid the diner's closed, and so is the coffee shop, so there's no place to eat."

He brushed his knuckles down her cheek and she shuttered. "Cathy?"

"Yes?" she whispered.

"I don't want to go back to the inn and be alone right now. Can we just stay here for awhile, like this?" His heart picked up triple-time as he waited for her response.

"No."

He closed his eyes. "I understand."

"I'll do you one better. If you promise to be a gentleman, you can come to my house and I'll cook us something. I can't send you back to the inn on an empty stomach. After all, you did save the day here."

His body lightened, as if a chunk of the boulder on his shoulders had fallen to the floor. "I'd like that."

"Great. Let's head over before the ice gets any worse. My house is just up the street. I think we should just walk. Sheriff Mason has probably blocked off the street because of black ice already." Cathy slid from his arms then turned off the lights before leading him to the front door and locking up.

The sidewalk was already slick, so he took her hand and tucked it into the crook of his arm. "Let's take it slow and easy."

She shivered at his side and he wished he had a coat to offer her. "I guess I should've dressed warmer, but I've been so busy I didn't even check the weather this morning."

"Me either. I hope you have heat or a warm fire at your place," he teased.

"I've got both." She winked and led him down Main, past the dark coffee shop. They continued through the town square, a large park at its center, and crossed a side street.

"This is a beautiful tree-lined street. I was admiring it on my run the other morning. All those homes with their white picket fences and Victorian details are like something out of a movie. I once dreamed of living in a home like that."

"Really?" Cathy asked.

"Yes. It was a dream I thought Kimmie and I shared, but apparently that wasn't what she had in mind for her future."

Cathy snuggled closer to his side for warmth, or for comfort, he wasn't sure, but he liked it. "It sounds like your marriage had trouble from the start."

"Yeah, I guess it did. Looking back now, I realize a few things."

"Like what?" Cathy pointed to a massive crack in the sidewalk and he carefully stepped over the broken cement.

"You shouldn't get married just because you're expecting a baby. At least, not now. I guess back then there was no other choice. It's just not the way to start a marriage with someone you barely know."

"Ah, shotgun wedding, huh?" Cathy bumped her hip into his.

"Yes, it was a complete surprise. We had only been together once. I know that's all it takes, but I didn't expect it. Naivety of youth, I guess. It was my first time with a woman. She was more experienced and said we'd be fine. Of course, now I know better. I still wonder if she got pregnant on purpose for some reason. I knew her family was gone and she was lonely, but now I'm not sure."

They slowed in front of the home he'd noticed during his run. "Come on in. I'll prepare dinner while you start a fire and we can sit and chat while we eat and get warm. My fingers feel like popsicles and for the first time in my life, I wish I had a little more fat to insulate these aching bones."

"Please. You're perfect. Curvy in all the right places." He nudged her back with his own hip.

"Sir, I think you're hitting on me."

"I'd hope so, or I'm doing it wrong." He laughed and held open the wrought iron gate for Cathy.

She snickered as she passed, and smacked him on the shoulder. "Now, you promised to behave. I have weapons and I'm not scared to fire them."

"Like that mace?" The gate closed with a squeal and he followed her up the paver path to the front porch. He could imagine sitting on the front swing, sipping lemonade on a warm summer afternoon.

Cathy opened the door and flicked on a light. It only dimly lit the room, but provided enough light to see the antique furniture and beautiful things she'd collected over the years. The aroma of pine and cinnamon filled the air. A candle sat on a small table nearby, with what looked to have roots and cinnamon sticks stuck inside the wax.

"That's from the shop." She smiled. "Okay, firewood's over there and the lighter's on the hearth. Get to it, mister, while I preheat the oven. I'm afraid I don't have much, but I can bake a few pieces of chicken and some broccoli."

"Sounds perfect."

"Oh, and I have something for you." She opened her bag and handed him a semi-squished box. "I'm afraid it looked more appetizing before I crushed it."

He opened it to find a cupcake with icing smeared around the inside of the box. "It still tastes great, I bet." He stuck his finger into the frosting and tasted it. "Yum. I look forward to sharing this after dinner."

She sauntered into the kitchen when the rain started pelting against the window. "Looks like we made it just in time. I haven't seen a storm come on that fast in a coon's age."

He couldn't help but laugh. The woman was small town all the way to the bone and he liked it. She was someone who knew where she belonged, was strong, witty and full of life. A woman like that could keep a man's interest and not cause him to worry that she'd leave at the first sign of trouble.

He took firewood from the pile and stacked it onto the iron grate in the fireplace, stuffing newspaper underneath, along with a few pieces of kindling he'd found. The paper left black residue on his hands, so he brushed his palms on a cloth hanging from the stand of fireplace tools. Flames licked at the edges of the paper then engulfed each wad and the kindling.

The wind had picked up outside and he eyed the downpour, thankful his daughter wasn't still on the streets. Well, if what Sheriff Mason said was true.

The lights flickered and he turned to face the kitchen.

"Don't worry," Cathy called. "It's an old house and that happens sometimes. I guess I need to have some work done on the electrical." The distinct sound of the oven reaching temperature beeped. "I'll just stick these in here and then be right out."

With the fire handled, he sat on the hearth and warmed his hands.

The phone rang and Cathy picked up the corded receiver off the wall by the refrigerator. "Hello? Hi, Trianna. You doing okay? I'd hoped you'd be home by now."

Devon tried not to eavesdrop but he couldn't help it since the house was so silent. It had an empty kind of feeling and he tried to imagine Cathy spending her nights alone in such a big house.

"Okay. Well, I understand. Keep those animals safe and you don't need to be on the road anyway. I actually saw your fiancé setting out road closure signs. He's closing down the town then I'm sure he'll be home to you. You two behave. You aren't married yet."

Devon pushed a log into a better position.

"Bye, hon. See you tomorrow." She hung up then opened the pantry door. The lights flickered twice and went out. "Oh, darn. Well, I guess I better check the circuit breaker in the basement."

Devon went to the window. "No need. All the homes down the street are dark."

"That's a problem. Guess I need to find us some food we don't have to cook." The sound of cans shifting in cabinets and bags crinkling came from the kitchen. After several minutes, she said, "Okay, it's not much but it'll have to hold us over. We've got some beef jerky that Mason left, some granola bars, chips, and applesauce."

"Don't forget the cupcake. Sounds like a meal fit for royalty." Devon walked over and took the tray from her hands. "You're still trembling. Here. Sit by the fire." He grabbed an afghan off the back of a chair and wrapped it around her shoulders then sat on the couch by her side and rubbed her arms. "Better?"

"Much." Cathy eyed the fire. "I wasn't expecting it to be this cold before Christmas. I hope it lets up by morning."

"It's not looking too good. As soon as there's a break in the rain, I'll make a run for the inn," he offered.

"Well, if it's as bad as Trianna just claimed, you won't be able to walk back without freezing to death, or slipping on ice. I'll tell you what. You can spend the night in the guest room. But just remember, I sleep with a nine millimeter under my pillow, so don't try anything."

He held up his hands, a piece of beef jerky between his fingers. "I promise, I'll be on my best behavior. If not, you can kick me out into that sleet without another word."

"You bet I will." Cathy alternately nibbled on a granola bar and a piece of beef jerky then leaned back into the soft couch.

He ate two more chips then joined her, wrapping his arm around her shoulders. "This is nice."

She nodded. "It is. Tell me more about your ex. You were saying you had to get married."

"Yes. When we were together I thought it was a first time for both of us, but I quickly realized that wasn't the case. Right there, at that lie, I should've known something was wrong. I found out about six weeks later that she was pregnant, and we married two months after that."

"Were you unhappy all those years?" Cathy asked.

"Yes and no. Kimmie was younger than me, so I believe she wasn't ready to be a mother. At first, Becca was like a doll. Someone Kimmie could dress up and parade around in public. She loved being the center of attention and a newborn provided that for her. But when Becca started to grow up, that became an issue for Kimmie. She didn't like feeding, changing diapers, or spending any time at home. I tried to give her breaks. She'd go out with friends once a week for Mom's Night Out. Then one night, she came home earlier than usual and said she didn't like those women any longer and, more importantly, that she didn't love me anymore. I told her we'd go to counseling and that I was willing to work on our marriage, especially for Becca's sake. I was scared to death I'd lose my little girl.

Kimmie agreed to stay, but she wasn't around much after that. She started disappearing for extended periods and returned home only to ignore Becca and I. On Becca's thirteenth birthday, I'd had enough. I told her she needed to stay home more and be a mother and wife. That she was selfish and unfeeling to her own family." Devon leaned his head back against the couch.

"What happened?" Cathy whispered.

"She told me I wasn't a father and she should've never been a mother. Minutes later, she had her clothes packed and was out the door, never to be heard from again."

Cathy shook her head. "She never even wrote or called Becca?"

"No." Devon rubbed his temples to relieve the pressure.

"I can't even imagine walking out on my child. I'd do anything to see my kids and grandkids on a more regular basis. I don't understand how a mother could want anything less."

Devon shrugged. "I don't either, especially when it comes to Becca. She's an amazing dancer, she's so smart and everyone loves her."

"But then her mother left and everything fell apart?" Cathy asked.

"Yeah, that's about it." He walked over and stoked the fire, causing it to roar back to life. "I can't imagine why she's here in Creekside. She wanted nothing to do with us and now that I finally have the opportunity to speak to my daughter, she's going to swoop in and complicate everything. All I want is a chance to talk to

Becca and find out why she hates me."

"She doesn't hate you. She loves you. Trust me. I saw her eyes when you were in the coffee shop. I promise I'll try to get you two talking tomorrow. Perhaps you can work things out if you get to her first."

Devon turned and walked toward her. "You'd do that for me? You believe me?"

Cathy shrugged. "I'm usually a good judge of character and when you're not putting on a show, you're actually a good man." She shied away, a pink tinge spreading across her cheeks.

Dropping onto the couch beside her, he said, "At the risk of sounding showy, I think you're the most incredible woman I've met in a long time."

Cathy smacked his shoulder. "Oh, please."

He chuckled and snuggled her into his side. She rested her head against his shoulder. He felt warm and content. The house, the fire and the woman by his side was a dream come true. Somehow, he believed that if anyone could bring Becca back into his life, it would be Cathy Mitchell. He sighed and closed his eyes, leaning his head against hers.

For the first time in years, he dared to believe in someone and the possibility of a future.

CHAPTER ELEVEN

Cathy woke to smoldering embers in the fireplace, the smell of pine and cinnamon from the candle that had long since burned out, and the warmth of a man by her side. Her impulse was to run away screaming. The thought of a man spending the night at her home, even if nothing went on between them, was scandalous. Then she looked out the window and realized no one would even notice. They were all stuck inside, too.

"You're awake?" Devon asked, a sexy rasp to his voice.

"Yes. Did you sleep?" Cathy kept her head on his shoulder. They'd passed out in an awkward position and her neck and back were now in knots, but it was a small price to pay for a night of comfort and companionship.

"Not much, but I enjoyed watching you sleep." He pressed his lips to the top of her head and she snuggled in even more. His arm wrapped around her body and he squeezed her to his side. "That's the best night I've had in a long time."

Cathy felt heat rise in her cheeks, but refused to

look up at him. "Sure, it was. You've already told me about all the women you've..."

He stiffened by her side then leaned back and tilted her chin up to look at him. "Don't ever think this is anything like when I buried my sorrow with those women. I assure you the flings were mutual and I tried to never hurt anyone, but this is different. It's...real."

She didn't know what to say. A man had never paid her so much attention before and it was unnerving, in a good way. Was she falling for him? Could he actually be attracted to her?

He leaned in, his gaze capturing hers, his lips a few inches away. Her body thrilled with the idea of losing herself in his kiss, and things started to stir that hadn't stirred in decades.

"You're a beautiful, sexy and caring person, who any man would be lucky to have in his life." His lips parted as he came closer, but something inside her snapped.

She turned her head and leaned away. A feeling of guilt plagued her, but why? Her husband had been gone for a long time. Maybe it wasn't guilt, but fear.

"You okay? I'm sorry. I didn't mean to push you." Devon sat forward and ran his fingers through her hair, sending vibrations down her arms and back.

"It's not that." She sighed. "You're the first man I've been close to since my husband died. I'm not sure how to feel, but I can tell you everything in me wants to kiss you. My body longs for it, but my mind is stopping me. I'm always so sure of everything. But this is different."

Devon laid a finger on the side of her face and nudged her to look at him. "Then I'll wait. I have a feeling you're worth waiting for."

Cathy trembled at his gentle touch, his knuckles gliding to her neck and over her shoulder. "Let's concentrate on you and your daughter, and baby Amelia for now. We have to pull off a fundraiser tomorrow and a wedding the day after. We'll pick this up later."

"I think that's a great idea." Devon rose and offered his hand. "Is it still okay to hug you?"

"Is a spotted puppy in a wagon cute?"

Devon laughed. "I love that you always make me laugh. There's a lightness about you that cradles my heart and lifts it up."

She slid her arms around his waist and he enveloped her in a warm, strong cocoon of comfort and...*love*. Perhaps at her age feelings developed quicker because people had less time. It had taken more years than she cared to admit before she found this kind of feeling with Sam.

"Let's scrounge up some breakfast before we try to walk back. The sun's just coming up, but hopefully it'll melt the ice quickly."

"I glanced at the weather last night on my phone application Trianna set up for me and it should heat up fast." Cathy made her way to the kitchen and found some bagels and cream cheese. "I'm afraid coffee will have to wait until we get power back.

As if on cue, the lights flicked on. "I guess I'll make coffee then." She laughed. "If I didn't know better I'd think this town was trying to tell us something."

"What do you mean?" Devon asked.

"Oh, it's an old saying. Did you see the welcome sign on your way into town?"

"I think so. Why?" Devon walked up behind her and placed his hands on her waist.

"It says *where your heart and home belong*. Some believe that this town has a way of pulling you in, finding your happiness and keeping you here. It sounds silly, but that seems to be the case for most people."

"Can you give me an example?" Devon asked, moving to her side and leaning against the counter with that movie star flare he had.

"Well, Lisa came here, sight-unseen, to work at the antique shop with Judy. She had only ever talked to Judy through the Internet. Lisa came to hide out in this town after she'd gotten pregnant by an epic jerk. But she found Eric and made Sweetwater her home. Trianna came to town to search for clues about her brother's murder and ended up falling in love with the town sheriff, a man who swore he'd never marry again. Even James, who disappeared for decades and everyone believed to be dead, returned and married Judy."

Devon crossed his arms over his chest and studied the house. "Well, I hope I'm worthy of the town spell."

"I'm sure you don't believe in such nonsense." Cathy scooped grounds and poured them into the coffee maker.

"If it gives me a life with you and my daughter then I'll believe anything."

"Woo. What are you talking about? You just met me." Cathy absently brushed non-existent coffee grounds off the counter.

"True, but I know you're like no other woman I've ever met and that intrigues me. I know I want to stay long enough to get to know you, and if you're even half of what I see in you right now, I'm staying for good. Perhaps it's the Christmas season, but I'm hopeful."

Cathy closed the lid and flipped on the coffee pot. "I thought you weren't gonna lay it on thick any more, Mr. West."

He tugged her into his arms and gazed down at her. "I can make a Christmas wish. Anything can happen in a couple of days."

For a second, she thought maybe she could kiss him. She imagined the illusive toe-curling kiss women always went on about, the kind she'd never experienced, but something inside still kept her from moving too fast. She didn't believe he was playing her, but she still didn't fully trust him. She believed what came out of his mouth, but once he had his daughter back, would he change his mind? If he was a long time user of women, what would make him stop now?

"I see in your eyes that I've got a shot. Don't worry, though. I don't expect you to come around by Christmas, I'll give you all the time you need. I'm not going anywhere." Devon kissed her cheek. "Hey. Let me see those artistic pieces of yours."

"What? Why would you want to see those?" Cathy shook her head and moved to get coffee mugs from the cupboard.

Devon's eyebrows rose. "I'm a Humanities professor. Of course I want to see the art you've created."

Cathy snickered. "Art? Um, I doodle."

A large truck drove by, spraying sand onto the road.

"It looks like the county managed to get something to coat the roads with this morning." She set the two mugs beside the coffee pot, waiting for it to finish gurgling as the eye-opening aroma filled the kitchen.

"Let's have our coffee and bagels then I'll head back to the inn to get cleaned up and we'll open up the shop. Why don't you go ahead and shower and get ready. I'll wait here. Don't think I forgot about seeing your art, though."

"Sounds good, but I need a cup first. And give up on the art. I told you, no one's ever seen it."

Devon grabbed a mug and poured the moment the machine shut off and handed it to her. "You'll trust me some day. Now, hurry up."

"Thanks. It might take me a bit to get ready, though. It takes time to cover up the wicked queen of age."

Devon laughed. "I bet you look beautiful even with nothing on."

Her hand trembled and coffee sloshed in the mug.

Devon cocked an eyebrow at her. "I meant, without make-up, but I like where your mind went." He winked, causing that knee-weakening thing to happen again.

Darn him. She rested a hand on the counter, trying to act nonchalant, and took a sip of coffee to buy some time for her legs to start working again.

He tore off a piece of bagel and held it up for her to open her mouth. "There. You have sustenance and coffee. Now, go get ready."

She snagged her cell phone and made her way upstairs to clean up. At that moment, she wished she'd gotten more clothes when she went shopping with Judy. The kitty sweatshirts and old lady pants didn't fit her any longer. She wanted more calf-hugging boots and flattering sweaters. Of course, her budget dictated she best make do with what she had.

At the top of the stairs, she stopped and eyed a family picture. Once upon a time, she'd had children and a husband in this house. She ran a finger down the dusty frame and thought about the gift she once had. It was a good life, full of love. Perhaps someday she'd get an invitation to see her grandbabies, but for now it was time to move on with her own life and stop pressuring and guilting her kids into inviting her. Maybe by next Christmas they'd agree to come home for a weekend or something. But if they didn't, she wouldn't spend any more time mourning their loss. She'd raised them up to be strong and independent, and that was what they were. Now, it was time to move on to the next stage of her life.

The sound of dishes being washed caught her attention. No one but her had ever washed a dish in this house. She didn't know men knew how. With a grin, she sauntered into her bedroom and found a sweater that Devon hadn't seen her wear, leggings and her goulashes. At least it would be practical.

After showering, she saw she'd missed a message from Judy.

All is fine. Be home Christmas Even. Thanks for all your support. I'll explain her diagnosis further when I see you.

Cathy wanted to call, but knew the message didn't invite it. There was a time she wouldn't have cared about boundaries, but now she had other things to focus on. And she could do more good here than waiting at the hospital. She wanted to have everything set for the fundraiser and donor matching program before Judy returned.

I need to get to work.

After drying her hair and primping for at least thirty minutes, she went back downstairs to find Devon snoozing on the couch. "Hey you, I'm ready. I didn't know I took that long."

Groggy, he pulled himself upright to face her. Then his eyes snapped wide and he let out a whistle. "You look mighty fine, lady. Can I walk you into town?"

She shook her head. "I guess it takes a while for a leopard to change its spots."

"If you're expecting me to give up complimenting you, you can forget it. I have a feeling you haven't been receiving many lately and I'm making it my personal mission to make up for that." Devon snagged his jacket from the back of the couch then took Cathy's coat and held it up for her. She slid her arms in and Devon lifted her hair over the collar then pressed his lips to that sensitive part at the nape of her neck.

A jolt of something powerful woke her body.

Instead of pulling away, this time she rested her head back against his chest and held his hands around her middle for a second. She could stand there all day, but it wasn't an option, not with Judy returning soon.

"Okay. Let's go." Cathy opened the door, spotted the ice on the stairs, and closed it again. She wasn't going to have a repeat of the winter of 1994, when she took a clown-like slide down the front steps and landed in an unladylike position in the front yard. "I'll be right back." She scooted past him and snagged the salt from the kitchen pantry. The large blue container would just about do it.

With a tentative step, she walked out onto the porch and poured salt across the first step then held the banister and tried it. Sure enough, it worked pretty well. Step by step, she salted and made her way down. The ice was still thick along her front walk, but they managed to make it to the street, hand in hand, where they decided the sanded asphalt was a lot safer than the sidewalk.

At the edge of town, he pulled her into his arms and kissed her forehead. "I'll miss you. But most of all, thank you for trying to talk to Becca for me. It means the world to me to have someone, a woman, to help."

Cathy stood on her tiptoes and brushed her cheek against his. "I'll do my best." A hint of cologne remained and her body took over her mind for a second, drawing her lips to his neck. She pressed a kiss to his warm skin. He held her tight against him and sucked in a long breath. Her arms and legs trembled at their closeness. She raised her head and hovered her lips near his. White clouds from their shallow breaths joined between them teasing Cathy's resolve, until a car honked and broke the spell.

He released her. "I guess we should get out of the street."

Cathy sloshed up toward the café without facing him, positive her cheeks were flaming. "I'll come by the inn when I'm done speaking with Becca."

As Devon's footsteps faded into the distance, she eyed Café Bliss. It was already lit up and she hoped Becca had the morning shift. Trudging to the front door, she kicked the sandy ice from her goulashes before entering.

"I see you didn't take my warning." Becca stood in the center of the shop with a rag in her hand, eyeing Cathy.

"Hi, Becca. It's good to see you, too." Cathy slipped her coat off and took a seat at a nearby table. No one else wanted to brave the roads this early, so she'd have a chance to talk to Becca in private. "I think I'll have one of those peppermint mochas. Lite, with no whip, please."

Becca put on a fake smile. "Certainly. My pleasure."

The aromas of brewed coffee, nutmeg, and fresh baked pastries soothed Cathy's nerves, but one look at Becca warned this wasn't going to be easy. The sound of clanking tin pitchers and spoons echoed through the empty café. For a second, Cathy worried Becca might christen her drink with her own special sauce.

Watching her out of the corner of her eye, she saw

Becca slam a spoon down, gripping it so tight it bent slightly. The girl looked down and sighed. Holding both ends, she managed to return it to its original shape. Then she flipped her hair back, marched over to Cathy, and set the drink firmly down in front of her. "Here. I made it to go. And it's on the house, so you can be on your way."

"Boy, you must not get many tips with that sour attitude," Cathy said.

"I only have an attitude for meddling old women who won't mind their own business."

Cathy pushed her chair back and stood, hands on her hips, ready to hog-tie that little back-talking child. "You ever heard about respecting your elders? I might be old, but at least I'm not a hostile little brat who doesn't know a good thing when it's there. Now, you can just relax because a little temper tantrum isn't enough to drive this old bird out."

Becca stomped and huffed. "I can't believe him. Hasn't he done enough? Now, he has to sic you on me?"

"What has he done besides raise you, take care of you after your mother ran out, and search over several state lines in hopes to bring you home?"

"He lied to me. My entire life was a lie." Becca threw the rag down on the table and slumped into a chair. Rubbing her temples, she closed her eyes. "I don't owe him anything. Why doesn't he just leave so I can figure out who my real family is?"

Cathy pulled a chair up next to her and smoothed some hair away from her face. "You're not making any sense, child. What do you mean, who your real family is? Devon's your real family."

"No, he's not. I overheard him and my mother arguing one night over the phone. She said he'd never been my father. I found a document in her old file box. It showed who my real father was. A Mark Brenson."

"Mark Brenson?" Cathy hissed.

"Yes...you know him?"

Cathy glanced away, trying to decide how much she should tell the girl. "He was Lisa Gaylord's fiancé. When she became pregnant, he dumped her. Tried to force her to give the baby up."

"Just like he did my mother." She sighed. "That's when my parents got married."

Cathy thought back to what they'd discovered about Mark. He had gotten women pregnant before but bribed them to get abortions. He was the lowest form of the male species.

Becca quirked her head to the side. "You're not surprised by this, are you?"

"I wish I could say I was, but it fits Mark Brenson's MO. Is that why you were in New York?"

"Yes, but he denied I was his."

Cathy shook her head. "Maybe you're not. Maybe you really are the daughter of Devon West. That paper you found could have been anything. You shouldn't jump to conclusions."

Becca shook her head. "When I overheard my mother talking about my dad not being my biological father, I had a paternity test done." Tears streamed down her face. "He's not my biological father."

Cathy's head spun, her brain flipped through all

the information Devon had told her. Nothing led her to believe he knew that he wasn't the father. Certainly, he would've mentioned that fact. "Becca, I'm not a hundred percent sure, but I don't think your dad knows he isn't your biological father. People say things in the heat of the moment. I've spent a few days with him and he's never mentioned anything about you not being his."

Becca eyed her suspiciously. "You're just saying that because you want me to feel bad for him so I'll talk to him, but it won't work."

Cathy grasped both of her hands. "I do want you to talk to him, but you have to make that decision on your own. But before you do, think for a minute. Has your dad ever indicated he knew about you not being his biological daughter? Trust me when I say, I don't believe he has a clue."

Her face scrunched then her mouth dropped open and she gasped. "I...I don't know. All this time I was so sure he knew and that he had lied to me, but you might be right. He never gave any indication that I wasn't his. Could he really not know? Did my mother lie to him all that time?" A hint of remorse sounded in her voice.

"It's possible, based on what limited information I have about your mother. I'm not sure why she ran out on you guys, and you may never know, but you need to talk to your father."

Becca bit her nails and scanned the window. Rays from the rising sun seeped through the dark clouds, shimmering off the icy street. "No, I can't. Not yet. Promise me you won't tell him. I need more time."

"Why? Time for what?"

"I need to figure out if I really do have a sibling in this town. If so, I don't want my father getting involved. Not yet."

Cathy gasped.

"What is it?" Becca scooted forward to the edge of her seat.

"You're related to Amelia Gaylord, Lisa and Eric's baby."

"I know. That's why I'm here and chose to work a few doors down from Lisa. To get to know her so that..."

"So that you can be part of a family again," Cathy finished for her.

The front door opened and Rusty entered. He removed his hat and coat, eyeing Rebecca with more than a friendly good morning.

Cathy grasped the girl's knees to keep her seated. "Wait. There's something you need to know. Amelia's ill. She needs your help. You might be the only one that can save her."

"What's wrong? What can I do?" Becca asked.

Please, dear Lord. Let her help save Amelia. This will make everything right, Cathy prayed. "She has leukemia and might need a bone marrow transplant. From what I've read, a sibling has the best chance of being a match. Becca, you were brought to this town for a reason."

Becca rolled her eyes. "I don't believe in divine intervention, if that's what you mean."

"We call it *town intervention*. This county

possesses mysterious powers. That's what I believe, anyway. It tends to draw those we need the most to join our town family."

"Did you forget to take your crazy meds this morning?" Becca laughed.

"You can believe me or not, I don't care, but would you be willing to be tested to see if you're a match to Amelia?"

Becca glanced at Rusty who sauntered past, strutting like a peacock looking for a mate then waited at the counter for her. "Yes. She's the only family I have left."

Cathy shook her head. "No, darling. Your father's right by your side and he's not leaving. He may not be blood, but he's been there for you your entire life, and he'll continue to stand by your side, even if your mother doesn't want him to."

"It's not that I don't want him to," Becca mumbled. "I just can't right now. I've been mad at him for so long, but now...I don't want to hurt him. Promise me you won't tell him that I'm not his real daughter. Not yet. I just need time and then I'll tell him myself."

Cathy didn't like this. She leaned back in her chair. "I don't know. I've grown fond of your father, and he has the right to know. You need to tell him soon before he finds out some other way."

"How else would he find out?" Becca asked.

Your mother.

The thought of Devon's wife being in town was reason enough to be concerned, but if she told Becca, would it change anything or make things more confusing for the girl? That was something she needed to talk to Devon about. Perhaps if he came to speak to her, to tell her about her mother being in town, it would open dialogue between them. "Okay. I'll keep it to myself for a few days, but then I'm telling him if you haven't."

"Deal. I promise I'll tell him as soon as I find out for sure if Amelia's my sibling or not."

"If Mark Brenson really is your biological father, then Amelia's your half-sister. And if you agree to the bone marrow test, I know you'll be a match."

"It would be a great way to be welcomed into their family. They couldn't turn me away if I'm the match for Amelia."

Cathy knew she should set her straight. Tell her that being a donor wouldn't make a difference. Lisa, Eric, Judy and James would all welcome her to the family no questions asked, donor or not. But something kept her mouth shut. Would Becca still agree to the test and bone marrow transplant if she knew it wasn't necessary?

Cathy struggled between hiding the truth and saving Amelia. She would do anything to save that little baby, but was it right to keep so many secrets?

This was her chance to help Judy, wipe the slate clean. She knew Judy had forgiven her for keeping James' secret for so long. Would she forgive her again? This would all work out. It had to. She'd save Amelia and reunite Devon and Becca. It was what she was born to do.

CHAPTER TWELVE

Devon paced the inn's lobby, waiting for Cathy to arrive. The white sheer curtains over the front windows fluttered each time the heat kicked on. A soft melody played from the kitchen, low enough that he could still hear the hum of the radiator beneath the window. The old house creaked with each wind gust, making him jump at the smallest noise. Patience was never something he was good at.

Taking a deep breath to calm his nervousness, he eyed his phone, willing Cathy to call, but nothing. He rounded the couch once more and stared at the door until he couldn't take it any longer. Why did he send Cathy in his place? He needed to be there.

He snagged his coat off the walnut coat tree and swung the door open to find Cathy standing on the front porch, shivering. "What are you doing out here?" Devon asked, before he pulled her inside and shut the door against the freezing wind.

Cathy only shrugged.

His heart fell. *So, it's true. Becca hates me.* He ran a hand through his hair and collapsed onto the floral-patterned loveseat. "I get it. Thanks for trying. She didn't even speak to you, right? That's what she does. Just blocks everyone out."

Cathy's hand rested on his shoulder. "We had a conversation. She's coming around, but needs a little more time."

Devon swung to face her, his feet knocking into the coffee table, causing a ceramic vase to teeter. "Are you serious? She actually said she needed time? Not that she wanted me gone and out of her life?" Hope filled him, like a little kid on Christmas morning, waiting for a shiny, new bike.

Cathy walked around the chair and sat on the sofa beside him. He took her hand and kissed it several times. "Thank you. You have no idea what this means."

Her gaze traveled to the floor and his hope faded a little. There was more and whatever it was, she was reluctant to tell him.

"I don't know how long it'll take, and she didn't say she would speak to you, but let me keep working on her. I think she just needs time."

"Time I can handle. I can take that job at the community college, or heck, I could retire. It doesn't matter. I have enough saved. I've only worked so long to avoid the loneliness of an empty house. I know that sounds crazy."

"No, I get that." Cathy squeezed his hand. "I kept busy all these years to avoid being alone, too. It's tough to be without a partner."

Devon scooted forward. "Then give me a chance. Let me court you. I'll treat you like no other man ever has. You're everything I've ever wanted in a woman.

You're kind, tough, passionate, and honest. Those qualities are so difficult to find together in one package. Most of all, I enjoy being with you. It doesn't matter if we work in the shop, eat, or fall asleep in front of the fireplace. I've enjoyed every minute with you."

Cathy slipped her hand from his. "Don't you go putting me on a pedestal, now. I'm too heavy and it's likely to break, and then where would we be?"

Devon laughed. "You've no idea how beautiful you are, do you?" He leaned forward and placed a hand on each knee. "That just makes you even more attractive. I promise I'll be the perfect gentleman. I think I proved that last night. You're the kind of woman a man respects and adores. You are not and never could be a one-night stand. I want to be the man I know I was supposed to be before I became so sour. Give me a chance to be that man. You inspire me to be a better human being."

Cathy toyed with a loose thread on a throw pillow at her side. "I think you do the same for me. I'm no angel, trust me. I drive most people crazy. But with you, I'm more relaxed and not so impulsive. I want to think things through, instead of always pouncing." She exhaled heavily. "You need to know that I'm just as broken, or possibly even more broken than you. I don't know that I can be this person you see me as."

"You already are that person. The one person in this world that's all the things I need. I can see a future I've longed for my entire life, and I believe with you by my side, it's finally possible. Perhaps you're right, this town does have some sort of secret power to bring people together. Let's just take it one day at a time. We'll promise to be honest with each other and communicate about things so that we keep each other straight."

Cathy nodded. "I'd like that."

Her words filled him with enough adrenaline he thought he could run thirteen miles in the freezing rain and still feel like he was twenty-five again. "Good. It's settled. So then, what's on your agenda today? Is there anything I can help with?"

"I'm going to meet with Karen and Susan about the fundraiser and then I'm going to head over to the hospital to talk to Dr. Hendricks about the bone marrow screening. Why don't you go speak with Sheriff Mason about the police department getting involved? Then we could meet for lunch."

"I'd be happy to. I'm just sad we have to part ways. I'll have to get a hug before I go though." He stood and opened his arms, wishing he could kiss her and make love to her, but he knew restraint was essential with Cathy Mitchell. She was a woman of character and if he won her love, he knew it would be forever.

Her head tucked under his chin and her frame fit perfectly into his.

"Until later." He released her.

"Until later." She stepped away then slipped out the front door.

He hesitated, wanting to reach for her, for one more embrace, but she'd already reached the bottom step and was headed in the opposite direction. He shut the door and shuffled down the street toward his car.

The sheriff would be willing to assist with the fundraiser, he was sure of that. His job would be easy. Cathy, on the other hand, had a much more challenging job ahead of her.

He reached his car in the back parking lot, a sting on the back of his neck made him spin to see who was behind him. Only a squirrel, skittering across the cold asphalt, no doubt searching for a hideout from the cold. Still, he scanned the few people at the edge of the lot, preparing to begin their day, but there was no sign of his ex.

With a heavy sigh, he climbed into his car and drove to the precinct. As he headed for the front of the building, he tightened his coat around his middle to block the icy breeze. The glass doors were decorated with spray snow, cling-on snowmen, and other holiday icons.

A man exited, holding the door open for Devon. He quickly stepped inside and found a deputy behind the front desk.

"Can I help you, sir?"

"Yes, please. I'd like to speak to Sheriff Mason. Is he here?"

The deputy picked up a phone. "May I ask your name, sir?"

"Devon West. He won't know me, but I'm here to speak with him on behalf of Cathy Mitchell."

The deputy nodded and pressed a button. "Susan? Is Sheriff back there? There's a gentleman named Devon West who'd like to speak to him. Says Cathy Mitchell sent him."

He lowered the receiver. "Just a second. She's checking with Sheriff Mason to find out if he has a few minutes."

"Thank you." Devon leaned against the counter and eyed the shrub of a Christmas tree in the corner. The star on the top reminded him of the one on the town clock, and on the tree at J & L antiques. Creekside showed their Christmas spirit in and on every building.

The deputy angled the receiver back to his mouth. "Great. I'll tell him." He hung up. "He'll be right out. You can have a seat over there, if you'd like." The deputy pointed to two grey chairs in the corner.

"Thanks, but I'll stand." Devon paced the waiting area to keep warm. The smell of bitter coffee and pine drifted throughout the room, along with a faint odor of disinfectant. He glanced out the front doors, still feeling uneasy. Was Kimmie really watching him? Why would she even bother? She had made it clear she didn't want anything to do with him when she walked out of their lives.

His gaze drifted to the thick metal doors behind the reception desk and he realized the precinct probably had holding cells in the back. It was still hard for him to comprehend that his ex-wife had spent time in a cell somewhere. Try as he might, he just couldn't imagine his vain ex-wife wearing the drab jumpsuit of a correctional facility.

One of the metal doors in the back popped open and Sheriff Mason stepped out. He stood tall, with a little silver lining his dark hair. The man had an honest face and he smiled when he saw Devon. "Hello, Mr.

West. It's a pleasure." He extended his hand and Devon took it to exchange a firm handshake. "Please. Follow me back to my office. We'll be more comfortable there."

"Certainly." Devon followed him through the door and into a sterile hallway. They walked past the two empty holding cells and turned left into a hall of offices. Back here, the disinfectant smell overpowered all the other aromas in the building. That, coupled with the plain white cinderblock walls, reminded him of the hospital where he'd had his appendix removed a few years back.

Sheriff held out his hand, gesturing to Devon to have a seat while he took the chair behind the desk. "So, what can I do for you? Susan mentioned something about Cathy. She's an amazing lady. And she never really asks for anything, so I have to admit, I'm intrigued."

Devon sat forward, resting his elbows on his knees. "I assume you know who Amelia Gaylord is?" Sheriff Mason's face grew pale. He must've known something was going on with the baby. "They, uh, they received the news that she has Leukemia."

He heard a gasp behind him. "Oh, dear lord in heaven."

Devon turned to see a woman standing in the doorway, a hand cupped to her mouth.

"This is Susan, my secretary," Mason said.

Wait. Didn't Cathy say she was going to talk to a Susan? He cringed, feeling guilty for being so blunt. He knew Cathy would have handled it better.

He nodded to her, but she remained transfixed, a

pleading look on her face, as if the sheriff could arrest this nasty culprit.

Devon cleared his throat. "I'm sorry to bring such bad news, but Cathy wants to help."

Sheriff Mason took a long breath. "I'd expect no less from that woman. Tell me what she needs."

"She wants to set up a fundraiser with some sort of big shopping day here in town to help pay for the astronomical costs of treatment and also get the word out that Amelia needs a bone marrow donor, not to mention a few other things. I'm not sure what all she wanted from you exactly, but I told her I'd come speak to you. She's meeting with a Karen and Susan to work on getting the word out. Something about the church."

"Yes. Karen's the church secretary." Mason steepled his fingers then rested his chin on his hands.

"I think they'll be planning a fundraising event with the church."

"Ah, I see." The sheriff glanced at Susan.

"I'm on it." She pulled a notepad and pen off Mason's desk and disappeared just as quickly and quietly as she'd come.

Devon looked between them, feeling as if he'd missed something.

"Don't worry. I know what Cathy's asking for," Mason assured him. "She'll need help expediting permits and making a few other things happen in town. Tell her that, for her, I'll do anything."

Devon nodded. "Thank you."

He leaned back in his chair and smiled. "By the way, word in town is that you're interested in our Cathy

Mitchell. You've been seen dining with her and I know you were at her house last night. You're one lucky man. She's a good woman."

Devon smiled. "I know. I asked her if I can court her and she said yes, so I hope to be staying in Creekside for a while."

The sheriff leaned forward, his chair squeaked loudly beneath him. "There's one more thing. From what I understand you're Becca's father and you're hoping to reconnect with her."

Devon swallowed hard. "Yeah, but I assure you there won't be any trouble. Cathy spoke to her just this morning and she's thinking about reuniting with me. She's been troubled for years, but I think this town has been good for her."

"What kind of trouble?" The sheriff's tone turned more interrogative than inquiring.

Devon shook his head. "Nothing of that sort. It's more that she's been in some sort of depression or something. She went from a star athlete and straight A student to running away from home. She's never been in jail or anything. From what I understand, she's been working two jobs and doesn't have time for any nonsense."

"Mrs. Fletcher, the owner of Café Bliss, says she's a good girl who just fell on bad times, but she's a hard worker and great kid."

"Yeah. I just wish I knew what caused her the hard times."

Mason cocked an eyebrow. "You still don't know?"

Devon traced a finger over the cracked varnish on

the sheriff's desk. "No. I have an idea, but nothing substantial."

The sheriff stood and offered his hand. "Well, I hope you're able to figure it out soon."

"So do I."

Mason kept hold of his hand. "You sound like you don't believe it will happen."

"It's not my daughter," Devon said, looking him in the eye. "It's her mother."

The sheriff released his hand and leaned a hip on the desk, crossing his arms over his chest. "What about her?"

Devon rubbed his throbbing temple. Even the idea of her made his head hurt. "She left without a word when Becca was thirteen, which is what I believe sparked my daughter's challenges. I recently discovered her mother served time, got released two months ago, and now she's here in Creekside. I saw her yesterday. Didn't actually talk to her, but I'm positive it was my ex-wife, Kimmie. I'm afraid she'll confront Becca and send my daughter running from town and I'll lose her again, possibly forever this time. I'm not sure why she'd even want to see Becca. She abandoned us and never looked back. But her being here at the same time as Becca is too much of a coincidence."

Sheriff Mason tilted his head. "People can change, you know. Maybe jail time set her straight and she just wants a chance to try again."

Devon swallowed. "Perhaps, but if she had, why didn't she call out to me when she saw me, instead of running off? I feel like she's been watching me, too. It sounds paranoid, I know, but I'm just afraid for my daughter."

The room remained silent for a few moments before Sheriff Mason straightened. "I tell you what. If you can provide a picture, I can have my men keep an eye out for her. If we spot her, we can at least ask her what she's doing in Creekside."

"You would do that for me?"

Sheriff Mason touched Devon's shoulder in a friendly gesture and led him from the room. "I'll do it for my town and Cathy. You, I don't know yet. I'm hoping you're a man of your word and have the best of intentions. We'll see."

Devon admired the man and his ability to command without disrespecting.

When they reached the metal door they'd entered through, the sheriff paused. "Devon, send that picture as soon as possible. If you're right and you're ex-wife's really in town, one of my men may have already seen her. He reported seeing a woman he didn't recognize standing outside the café the other night, looking through the windows. When he approached her, she fled. From her behavior, I suspect she's waiting for an opportunity."

Devon froze. "An opportunity for what?"

"I'm not sure. That's what concerns me. I believe she's waiting for a chance to speak to your daughter or you alone. In my experience, when someone won't be upfront, it usually means they're hiding something."

"Like what?"

"I don't know, but they'll do anything to keep from

getting caught, and take down anyone who gets in their way."

CHAPTER THIRTEEN

Cathy walked into the recreation center and set down one of the boxes of cupcakes Karen had told her to carry. Frank shuffled over and reached out to snag one, but Cathy slapped his hand. "I don't think Karen will be too pleased if you go stealing one of those. They're for after bingo."

Frank massaged his hand and stuck his lip out, looking like a dog who'd been smacked with a newspaper. "Didn't have to hit me. I'd turn you over my knee and spank you for being rude, but the sheriff'd probably arrest me again."

Trianna dropped a box of bingo cards and stamps next to the cupcakes. "We talked about that, Frank. No more touching the ladies. I don't want to have to ban you from our activities."

"I weren't touching no one. Besides, if it would stop my grandson from dropping me off here all the time like some preschooler, I'd be grabbing more—"

"Frank," Cathy scolded. "You better be nice or you'll be stuck inside that house of yours by yourself all day again. I know you, old-timer. You talk a good game, but you like being around people."

Frank waved at the air. "Ahh, you don't know what you're talking about," he said as he shuffled away.

Karen joined them and set a second box of cupcakes on the table.

Trianna clapped her hands together. "Oh, they look so delicious. You're amazing for doing this. I can't wait to taste them. Jimmy will be here soon, too. He's just finishing up something at the precinct. Thanks so much for agreeing to make the cupcakes for our wedding. I can't believe it's only a couple days away. There's still so much to do."

"It'll be amazing." Karen wiped her hands down the front of her apron. "Okay, I'll set up these and get a tasting tray ready for you and Sheriff Mason."

"You get away from me before I knock your teeth out!" Frank shouted from across the room.

"You're just jealous 'cause you ain't got no teeth."

Cathy looked up to see what the commotion was all about, but Trianna was already trotting over to break it up.

"Karen, how're you going to be able to make all the cupcakes for the wedding and for Amelia's fundraiser?" Cathy asked.

"Don't worry. I've already got a plan." Karen winked.

"What's that?"

Karen smiled mischievously and Cathy stepped back. That look was a telltale sign Karen was about to drop something big on her. "You're gonna help me."

"Me?" Cathy shrieked.

"If you want to pull this off by tomorrow, you best

whip out those baking skills. I'll be ready to start this afternoon by four. Plan on working until late, though."

"Fine. I'll be there at four." Cathy sighed. She hadn't baked in years, but having Karen do everything herself was too much to ask.

Sheriff Mason entered and waved before pulling Trianna in for a kiss that could cost him his position for violating public decency laws.

"Woo. The Sheriff's got game." Mr. Meyers yelled loud enough for most of the center to hear. The room exploded into laughter.

"See you at four," Cathy called as she headed for the door.

She drove back to Main and parked in front of J & L Antiques. With most people not willing to brave the cold or already over at the recreation center, there was no reason to open the store. So, after checking the doors, she walked over to the inn and waited inside the warm lobby for Devon to return.

"Good morning, Mrs. Mitchell," Mrs. Hatfield called out from behind the front desk. "How've you been?"

"Good. And you?"

"Great. It's been pretty quiet though, considering it's so close to Christmas, but I'm fully booked for Christmas Eve, thanks to the Shaw–Mason wedding. Then I'm closing up shop the day after Christmas and heading over to visit family in the Carolinas. Have I ever told you about my husband's family?"

"Yes, ma'am. Old lady Hatfield sounded like one mean son of a gun."

Mrs. Hatfield roared with laughter. "You got that right. When I went to marry her son, we had to lie and say I was knocked up. It was the only way we'd have gotten her okay."

"I hope you got pregnant quick then. Based on that gun she's holding in the portrait you've got there, she probably didn't take too kindly to liars."

"No. I'm afraid not." Mrs. Hatfield whistled. "She nearly got me one night when she shot up our bed. If I wouldn't have been sleeping on the couch 'cause I missed my husband so much when he was away, I'd be a dead woman. Eventually, I had little ones, but it took a year to get pregnant."

"And you want to go visit?"

The old woman smiled, her hair perfectly styled into a big silver helmet. "I put in my years. I'm one of them now." With that, she tottered off to the kitchen.

The door creaked open and a gust of cold wind hit Cathy, nearly turning her into a brick of ice in an instant. She spun around, but the lobby was empty. Wrapping her arms around herself, she held her coat tight then walked out onto the front porch. She heard the clicking of heels and caught a glimpse of a dark coat rounding the corner, but before she could go see who it was, Devon trotted up the steps.

"What are you doing out here?" he asked.

"The door flew open by itself, and I came to see what happened, I thought I saw someone."

Devon scanned the street, his eyebrows furrowed with obvious concern.

"What is it?"

He climbed the last step and pulled her into his arms. "Nothing. I just don't want anything to happen to you now that I've found you."

Cathy studied his face. Half-truth, half BS. She couldn't really accuse him of hiding something from her when she was doing the same thing. But that didn't mean she couldn't try prodding it out of him.

She snagged his hand and yanked him inside the inn. "Okay, Devon West. Spill it."

"Why do you think—"

Cathy shook her head. "Honesty. Remember? If not, I'm out of here."

Devon sighed. "I think it's my ex-wife. Sheriff Mason's concerned she's here for a reason and whatever it is, it isn't pleasant. I've been scared for Becca, but now I'm a little concerned for you, too. What if she has some crazy notion that I'm still hers? I mean, she's always been difficult to handle, but now that she's served time... I guess I'm just not sure what to think. I'm probably just being paranoid." He rubbed small circles into his temple. "I emailed an old picture of her to Sheriff Mason a little while ago. He promised that if they see her, they'll try to talk to her."

"Then there's nothing to worry about. Jimmy's darn good at his job. Pretty much guaranteed to get re-elected." Cathy slid her fingers into his. "See? That wasn't so hard."

"No. Not with you anyway." Devon leaned forward and planted a quick kiss on her lips. A heat ran through her, causing the shivering to stop. He literally heated her from the inside out. "I hope that wasn't too forward."

It wasn't forward enough. I want a real kiss this time. Cathy shook her head. *What's wrong with me? I'm turning into a little hussy.* "It was fine."

"Just fine?" Devon pouted. "I guess I need to try harder."

"I look forward to it." Cathy glanced at Mrs. Hatfield who was leaning over the front desk, trying to hear their conversation.

"Mrs. Hatfield, we're doing an impromptu fundraiser tomorrow afternoon to benefit little Amelia Gaylord. The weather's supposed to be clear and they'll be a lot of out-of-town shoppers coming in for the Christmas sale we normally hold. If you can help, please let me know."

Mrs. Hatfield came around the counter. "I can open the inn for some refreshments and whatnot for someone to sell. Feel free to use the lobby. I can also charge a tour fee and show folks the old antiques, letters, and pictures from the Hatfields, like I did when we held the fundraiser for that young man who was injured in Iraq."

"That sounds perfect. I'll put it down on the flyer. Thanks so much." Cathy waved and left with Devon at her side for the diner. But instead of heading left, he tugged her toward the right.

"Where are we going?" Cathy asked.

"To a little restaurant in the next town. I think it's time we had a proper date. And I have a feeling there are too many prying eyes around here."

Cathy liked the way his hand slid protectively to

the small of her back, guiding her to his car. He opened the door for her and even made sure she was tucked safely inside before closing it.

The leather seat was cold beneath her. She blew on her hands and looked up through the windshield. A thin sheet of ice coated the glass, even with the sun's rays now shinning between the clouds. Through the side window, she noticed a woman with dark hair standing at the corner of the next building over, watching them.

When Devon got in, Cathy pointed. He looked up and his mouth fell open. "Wait here," he said, reaching for the door handle.

Cathy grabbed his arm. "No. I'll call Sheriff Mason. If she's unstable, you don't know what she's capable of." But before she could even retrieve her phone, the woman vanished.

"Let's go. I'll text the sheriff while you drive and send Rusty to the café to keep an eye on Becca. He's not able to work today because of the weather anyway."

As Devon started the car and pulled out of the parking lot, Cathy typed out *Devon's ex spotted near inn. She disappeared again*, and hit *send*. Then she scanned her contact list and found Rusty. *Please hang at café and keep an eye on Becca. There's something going on. Text me if any strangers come. I'll be happy to pay for your time.*

Her phone dinged as they turned onto the road toward Riverbend and she glanced down. "Sheriff Mason dispatched the deputy on duty to check it out and he's headed that way, too."

"Thank you. I wish I could protect her," Devon mumbled. "But she'll just think I'm interfering again."

"I know, but this is for the best." Cathy covered his hand with hers.

He lifted their joined hands and kissed her palm. "Thank you. I can't believe you're so helpful. I never thought I could trust another woman again. I'm so lucky to have you helping me. Most woman only care about what they can get out of a relationship. Money, prestige, favors or whatever else they can manage. You're the first woman to ever do me a favor without asking anything in return. You truly are a gift."

Her stomach rolled with the knowledge of her deception. She was tired of keeping secrets. It nearly killed her to keep the truth about James from Judy for so long, yet here she was doing it again. While she knew the truth about Becca would hurt him, he deserved to know. She needed to tell him, but she couldn't without losing Becca's trust. And she needed that trust, not only for the sake of reuniting them, but for little Amelia's sake.

After waffling back and forth, she realized she just couldn't betray the man at her side. She opened her mouth, but her cell phone cut her off. Her heart beat like a bass drum in one of those rap songs. "It's Rusty," she said, feeling slightly relieved to be getting off the hook. "He said he'd be happy to watch out for Becca, but I'm not allowed to pay him." She chuckled. "I think he's a little sweet on her."

The car swerved but Devon quickly recovered. "Who's this boy?"

"Calm down. Rusty's a fine young man. Hardworking and single-handedly takes care of his grandfather, who doesn't always make it easy for him. Trust me. Becca could do much worse. Besides, she's nineteen and estranged from you. What're you going to do about it? Go into Café Bliss with a shotgun and threaten him?"

"Maybe." Devon pressed his lips together.

"Well, before you go doing anything stupid, you should know his grandfather got a shot off on the assailant that tried to kidnap Trianna. I may have taken out his getaway car but Frank was the one to save Trianna. He's a crazy old coot, so you best be civil to his grandson."

Devon remained silent until he pulled into a parking space in front of a nice mom-and-pop diner in Riverbend. "I hear the food's good here, and even better, I have you all to myself." He hopped out and opened her door. Always the gentleman, he opened the door to the restaurant as well and even pulled out her chair at the table.

The aroma of grilled steak and onions filled the room. Cathy laid the thick cloth napkin on her lap. "Smells delicious."

"Yeah, I'm looking forward to trying it. The diner in town's good, but it's nice to try something new."

After the waitress came to take their drink orders, Devon reached across the table and took her hand. "I don't know how I'd have handled all this stuff with Becca without you. Thank you for guiding me through it. I made so many mistakes after her mother left. I was a single father, trying to raise a young woman. I tried, but I know I failed. From the first moment I held her in the hospital, I couldn't believe that perfect little human being was a part of me. That I'd helped bring her into the world."

The look of wonder in his eyes at the memories tugged at Cathy's conscience.

"Her mother suffered from post-partum after she was born, so she slept a lot. I would get up at night to feed and rock Becca when she was a baby. Even when she was two or three, it was me she always called for if she had a nightmare. We were so close. After her mother left, she clung to me and we managed to get through it together, until the divorce papers arrived. I kind of knew it was coming. I mean, she'd been gone so long. I guess I assumed Becca was prepared for it, too. But it wasn't long after that she was gone and my entire world vanished in a single breath."

Cathy squeezed his hand. *This isn't fair.* He was going to be devastated when he learned the truth. That woman was evil for keeping these secrets and putting not only Devon, but Becca through all this. If she still had her Cadillac, she'd run that woman down and bury her some place in the woods where no one would ever find the body.

"If I only knew why. What caused Becca to runaway that night? Then I'd have a chance to make things right with her."

Cathy gripped the table with her other hand to keep from spilling the beans. She owed it to him, but she had to think of Becca and Amelia, too.

As soon as lunch was over, she was going to march into the café and demand Becca tell him the truth. If not, she'd tell him herself. She couldn't keep this secret a second longer. She'd make them both see that blood means nothing, that he was truly her father in every sense of the word, even if she had to hog-tie them and throw them in one of Sheriff Mason's holding cells for a week.

Nothing and no one would be able to keep them apart once they worked through this. They just needed to talk. After that, everything would be right as rain.

CHAPTER FOURTEEN

The morning sun peeked through the window, rousing Devon from a deep sleep full of dreams about love and family. Magic from a small town that brought him all the happiness of a home full of life faded as his eyes fluttered open.

He stretched his arms over his head and every joint in his body popped, but there wasn't any pain. He felt exhilarated and looked forward to helping with the fundraiser for baby Amelia. In the next twenty-four hours, he'd spend a lot of time with the people in Creekside between the fundraiser and the Christmas Eve party. It was a great opportunity for him to get to know people in town. If he wanted to stay in Creekside, he needed to find a home and get to know more of Cathy's friends. He knew how things worked, he needed to earn their approval if he was going to court her.

Slipping out from underneath the warm, quilted bedding, he quickly showered and dressed. He wanted to hurry and grab a cup of coffee from the café. It was an excuse to see Becca, but he didn't care. It would be the perfect way to start the day.

Just as the clock struck seven, he hurried down the stairs, planning to meet with a realtor before he headed to the recreation center to find out what his job would be for the day. The streets were mostly empty, save for a car or two that passed as he made his way across the street to the café. The icy chill had faded during the night, and even though the weather was cold, at least it was bearable now.

With her head buried in her phone, Cathy marched up the sidewalk and plowed into Devon. He caught her before she stumbled over. "Where you going in such a hurry?"

She dropped her hands to her sides. "Oh, I'm so sorry. I was just in another world. I've got so much to do, and let's just say things didn't start off so well." She cast a sideways glance at the café.

"Is there something I can do?" Devon asked.

Cathy took a deep breath. He knew she was under a lot of stress with the fundraiser, but it seemed like something more was bothering her.

"Go say *hi* to your daughter. Talk to her, then come find me at the rec center and tell me how it went." She cupped his cheek, her gaze softening into a sadness. Or was that pity?

"What's wrong? Is Becca okay?"

Cathy pulled him into a hug. "She's fine. Just remember people in this town care about you. Promise me that you'll come find me at the center right after you speak to Becca, okay?"

Devon eyed her for a moment, but he wanted to do what he could to set her mind at ease. He couldn't bear to cause her anymore undo stress. "Promise."

She smiled weakly then sidestepped around him and hotfooted it to her car.

He opened the door to Café Bliss to a burst of dry heat, but the aroma of fresh brewed coffee drew him inside. A tree covered with sparkly tinsel and red metallic balls decorated the corner, small wrapped packages tucked underneath. His pulse quickened at the sight of his daughter behind the counter. She looked good. A few faces he already recognized stood in line to order drinks or sat at tables. Warm smiles, friendly handshakes and hugs were exchanged every time he glanced around the small shop.

"Welcome," said a young man, possibly a senior in high school or freshman in college. He offered his hand. "I'm Marcus, and this is my girlfriend, Rose. We're home for winter break."

"Nice to meet you." Devon shook each of their hands and smiled. Marcus's Latin accent and dark features contrasted yet complimented Rose's pale skin and southern accent.

Devon glanced at his daughter behind the counter before turning back to the young couple.

"I just wanted to introduce myself after hearing so much about you from Rose. She and Cathy are close. Rose lived with her for a short time."

"Yes, I remember Cathy mentioning that." Devon glanced once more at Becca then shuffled toward the counter. "I'm so glad I got to meet you both in person."

"Same here. We'll see you over at the fundraiser." Marcus wrapped his arm around Rose and guided her to an empty table. The way Rose looked up at Marcus spoke volumes and Devon couldn't help feeling envious. They were the lucky ones. Having found their soul mate so young, they had the rest of their lives together.

Devon approached the register. To his relief, Becca didn't hide this time.

Staring straight into his eyes, she said, "What can I get for you?"

She actually spoke to me. Perhaps Cathy has made progress with her. His heart lifted with hope, soaring to the top of the Smokey Mountains in the distance. "I'll take a medium house blend coffee, please." Devon pulled cash from his pocket and paid, then dropped a twenty into the tip jar.

"Dad, you can't tip twenty bucks on a dollar coffee," Becca protested.

Devon shrugged. "I can tip what I want. I found the service to be exceptional. Becca rolled her eyes as he moved to the end of the counter to pick up his coffee.

She poured it, topped the cup with a plastic lid then handed it to him. "Hey, I heard you're going to be working at the fundraiser for Amelia."

"Yeah. Are you?"

Becca shook her head. "I wish, but I need to work today. Thanks for helping though. The Gaylords are good people. It breaks my heart that Amelia's sick. She's a special little girl." Her eyes shone with unshed tears. She must've become close to the Gaylords. Yet, there was something more in her eyes, a connection to that baby he didn't understand.

"Have a good day." Becca smiled, a real smile, one from before his ex had abandoned them.

He could only smile back. Too scared to say something and ruin the moment, he retreated to the cream and sugar station. After doctoring his coffee, he stole one more glance at his baby girl.

Mrs. Fletcher chatted with Becca behind the counter, each of them glancing at him. Curious, he stalled, wiping sugar granules off the counter and stirring his coffee one more time.

"Dad," Becca's voice sounded behind him. He swung around, attempting to hide the elation from his face, but by the way the muscles in his cheeks were twitching, he knew he'd failed.

Becca toed the tile grout on the floor and tucked a stray hair behind her ear. "Um, looks like I'll be able to join the fundraiser after all. Mrs. Fletcher's sending me with some donations and told me to stay and help until my shift ends." She peeked through the wayward hair that had already come loose again.

"That's great. I guess I'll see you there."

"Yeah. And if you have a few minutes, I want to talk to you."

He fisted his hands at his sides to keep from pulling her into a hug. "I have time now," he said hopefully.

Becca shook her head. "No, it needs to be later."

"Okay, I'll make sure I have time after. I have something I'd like to talk to you about, too, if that's okay." His pulse did a little dance in his neck, thumping with joy.

Becca nodded then returned behind the counter. Devon nearly skipped to the door, but forced a steady gait.

"Dad. You forgot something," Becca called out.

He looked to her and she pointed at his abandoned coffee, still sitting at the cream and sugar station. Heat rushed to his face. Without a word, he retrieved his cup and forced a smile before retreating out the front door.

The florist arranged a display of fresh flowers outside her shop and waved. "Good morning, Mr. West."

He returned the wave and crossed the street to the parking lot behind the inn. Mrs. Hatfield waved from an upstairs window and he nodded. Stealing one last look at the café, he saw Rusty drive up in an old beat up truck. Cathy was right. He did look like a hardworking lad. At Devon's wave, Rusty saluted and pulled into a spot in front of Café Bliss, no doubt to visit his daughter. Mixed feelings stirred inside him, but he knew better than to rock the bridge carefully being constructed between him and his daughter. Just like in a suspension bridge, each cable needed the support of hundreds of others, all tightly twisted together. Rusty, Cathy, and everyone else in this town, were the cables holding them up supporting them as they closed the gap in their relationship.

He took a quick sip of his coffee, instantly tasting the hint of vanilla. It wasn't just the hot liquid that warmed his insides, but the fact she'd remembered. They used to sit at the park every Saturday, him with his vanilla flavored coffee, her with a hot cocoa, feeding pigeons near the lake. It became their ritual until she turned ten and told him she wasn't a child any longer.

Becca had extended him an olive branch. Or more like a vanilla bean branch, though he wasn't sure vanilla beans grew on trees. But still, it was a peace offering. Deep down, he knew she'd told him she missed him in her own special way and that meant everything to him.

After placing his coffee safely in the cup holder, he drove to the realtor's office. He picked up the packet she'd left for him in the mail box outside and opened it with the same excitement as a package on Christmas morning. He felt impulsive, crazy and...alive. For the first time in years, it felt like a new beginning was about to start, instead of everything spiraling to the end.

Absently thumbing through the material, he paused by his car. The feeling of someone watching him caused the hair on the back of his neck to stand up again. He didn't have to look to know it was his ex. *Not today.* Not with Becca coming to work with him at the rec center. He wouldn't engage her. It would only open the floodgate of drama and trouble he knew she'd pour into their lives.

He hopped in his car and headed to the rec center. Not willing to risk his little bit of happiness, He took the long way, glancing in his rearview mirror every so often until he was sure she hadn't followed him. Even after his extra precautions, he still found a parking spot in the back, away from the sightline of the main road.

Many people were already filling the building. A

white van sat at the back door as several people unloaded boxes of goodies to sell for the fundraiser. He took a few swigs of coffee then stepped around them and into the rec center. Long tables lined the four walls, with several others joined together to make a rectangle in the center of the room. Ribbons, flowers and other adornments overflowed from various brown boxes scattered about the floor and the smell of baked goods filled the room with the aroma of Christmas. For the first time in years, Devon looked forward to the holiday...to the possibilities of what could be.

He spotted Cathy struggling to carry two boxes at once and hurried to her side. "Here. Let me get that for you."

Cathy happily relented, passing off one of the boxes. "Thanks. I could use a hero on a white horse about now."

"I'm happy to oblige, ma'am," he said in his slickest southern drawl.

Cathy laughed. The sound echoed through the room, completing the feel of a joyful holiday. "I think you best stick with your northern accent." She hip-bumped him then sashayed on ahead to guide him to a table at the other end of the room.

"You put all this together in only a matter of...what? Hours?"

Cathy shrugged. "It's what I do."

"Well, if I ever need something done, I know who to ask for help." Devon winked.

"I'd be happy to help you any way I can, sir." She winked back. He loved her confidence and southern charm. Her smile alone could melt his heart, but her desire to help others captured his soul.

"Put that right there." Cathy pointed to the ground next to three other boxes. "I only hope we can raise enough to help Amelia get better."

"I know. And I'm going to sound completely selfish, but this means even more to me. Please don't think bad of me, but Becca's coming. She said she wants to speak with me after the fundraiser. I'm glad, too, because I have something to tell her."

Cathy's right eyebrow arched. "What's that?"

Devon swallowed and took a deep breath. "I don't want to frighten you off."

She leaned into him and kissed his cheek, taking one of his hands in hers. "I don't think you can do that if you tried."

Devon squeezed her hand. "I picked up a packet from the realtor in town. I'm thinking about moving here." He held his breath, waiting for her to run from the building screaming at his forwardness.

"That doesn't surprise me. I mean, your daughter's here and all." Cathy released his hand, but he snagged hers to keep her from moving away.

"What if she isn't the only reason I want to stay?"

Cathy took two deep breaths, which felt like a lifetime, before she looked up and caught his gaze. A deep sadness crossed her eyes, but disappeared in an instant. He froze, waiting for her to say something.

"So, you decided on that job at the community college, huh? Have you looked at any homes yet? I might have some recommendations for you."

Devon slowly stepped back. "No, not yet. I only picked up the packet this morning. I'm sorry, if I've overstepped any boundaries. I guess—"

"You haven't, darlin'. I'm thrilled you'll be staying." The smile creased her cheeks once more, but it wasn't the kind that lit her eyes.

"Well, at least I'll know where to find you." His ex-wife's voice crawled down his back, digging tentacles of fear into his spine.

He slowly turned, his eyes narrowing on the one person who could steal everything from him, erase all the happiness he'd worked so hard for. He didn't know how she'd do it, but she would. Somehow, she'd destroy the little progress he'd made with Becca.

"Leave," he hissed.

Her once fragile beauty, with classic features, had been replaced with rough skin and fried hair. She waved her hand dismissively. "Oh, Devon. You were always so dramatic."

"I won't say it again. You leave, or I'll forget I'm a gentleman and physically remove you."

Cathy stepped between them, stretching out her hand. "Hi, I'm Cathy Mitchell. I thought I should introduce myself since I'm the organizer of this event. And as you can see, we could use your help here, Mrs.—"

"I know who you are. You're the woman who's trying to steal my husband."

"We're not married," Devon growled, "and haven't been for a long time. If it's money you want, leave now and I'll consider it."

"Oh, look. There's my daughter."

Devon spun on his heel, but even as he stopped, the room didn't. He knew, in that instant, his world was about to crumble...again.

CHAPTER FIFTEEN

Cathy sucked in a quick breath, spotting Becca in the doorway, her eyes wide and transfixed on her mother.

Devon clutched Cathy's hand tight, as though trying to keep himself grounded.

Spotting Marcus, she waved him over, hoping he'd read her facial expression and usher Kimmie out the door without a scene.

"I think it's about time we had a chat." As if relishing the growing tension, Kimmie sent Devon a sneer then sashayed toward Becca, but Devon sidestepped, blocking.

Kimmie huffed, but before she could maneuver around Devon, Marcus appeared at their side.

"Hi, there. I was wondering if you could help me with something." He layered on the Latino charm, like he'd just stepped straight off the cover of that Bruno Mars CD Rose always listened to when she'd been living with Cathy.

For a second, Kimmie faltered, staring up into Marcus's face as he took her hand.

Devon bolted to Becca's side, the movement

breaking Marcus's charismatic hold over Kimmie. Before she could dart after him, Cathy shuffled to block her path.

She snarled and Cathy had to resist the urge to backhand the woman. "I warn you. I'm not easily intimidated and right now, you're outgunned and outnumbered. It's time for you to leave."

"I think not," Kimmie snapped. "With one word, I can turn him on you and you'll learn how quickly he can betray a woman."

Cathy clasped her hands into fists. *I swear I'm going to send this woman back to the hole she's crawled out of.*

Kimmie eyed her fists. "What?" she asked, her voice raised. "My donation isn't good enough for you? I'm so sorry. I'm afraid it's all I can give today."

Cathy's mouth dropped open. Every pair of eyes around the room fixated on her. As she scanned the faces of her friends and family, Kimmie took advantage of the distraction and raced to Devon and Becca. Cathy quickly followed in her footsteps, trailed by Marcus, Rose and half the town.

"Hi dear, I've missed you." Kimmie opened her arms, but Becca backed away.

Devon stood in front of his daughter. "As you can see, Becca doesn't want you here either."

"Dad, it's okay. You've spent the last several years protecting me. It's time for me to grow up and deal with the truth."

A light shone on Kimmie's face. "Ah, the truth."

Cathy looked to Marcus and the rest of her friends,

in hopes someone could do something, but everyone stood around staring at each other, no doubt so they'd have something to talk about over coffee tomorrow.

"Yes." Becca squared her shoulders and stepped around her dad. "I've spent years trying to figure out what I did to ruin your life. That's what you said the night you left. You came in my room and whispered in my ear that I'd ruined your life. If you hadn't had me then you would've been free."

For a second, Kimmie's face twisted with remorse, but it didn't last. "If you had been asleep like a good little girl then you wouldn't have heard me."

"Are you serious?" Cathy didn't know Becca that well, but as a mother, she couldn't imagine ever telling a child such a thing. "You don't deserve to call yourself a mother. This young woman works two jobs, is always kind to others and is a beautiful human being."

"You're not family," Kimmie sneered. "Mind your own business."

"Well, neither are you," Devon said. "Would family walk out on their loved ones? What made you so bitter? I tried to be a good husband. Even when you made it difficult, I stayed and—"

"And what? Humored me? You're not a man. When I married you, I thought you'd take care of me and Becca. That life would be grand. You were well off and people adored you. A man I could show off on my arm. I thought I'd married well."

Devon's forehead grew red with anger. "That's all I ever was to you? An ornament and a paycheck? You closed the door on me shortly after Becca was born. But

I still clung to the idea of what could be. That was my mistake. Perhaps poor Becca wouldn't have gone through so much if I'd divorced you and taken her with me, and left you with nothing but an empty bank account."

Rusty walked up and dropped a box with a thud. "What's going on here? You okay, Becca?" He placed one hand on each of Becca's shoulders.

Becca leaned into him. "Yeah. I guess I should introduce you to my mother before she leaves."

"I'm not going anywhere. Not until I speak to my husband." An evil smile drew up at the corners of her mouth.

"Ex-husband," Cathy reminded her. She'd never wanted to choke someone so bad in her life. She was already plotting a map to that hole in the mountains.

"Technically, we're still married." She winked at Devon. "Silly me, I forgot to file some piece of paper so the divorce was never final. Isn't that great news? We can be one happy family again."

Becca shook her head, her gaze narrowing. Yet tears pooled at the corner of her eyes. Cathy had a sudden desire to pull Becca into her side to protect her. "You leave Dad alone. You've done enough to him. It took me a long time, but now I know that he only wanted the best for me. I'll testify in court if I have to. Tell everyone how you used my father for years until you found another victim. How you abandoned us, stealing half of his life-savings."

Devon gave his daughter a quizzical look.

Cathy quickly stepped in to divert the

conversation. "This isn't the place to settle this. Eric Gaylord is Mr. West's attorney. If you have anything more to say, you can contact him directly."

"No one asked you," Kimmie snapped.

Becca crossed her arms over her chest. "Don't talk to her that way. She's been more of a mother to me than you ever were."

Devon moved between Cathy and Becca, taking each of their hands in his. "You heard my ladies. It's time for you to leave."

"They're not your ladies! You're married to me, not her. And Becca is—"

"Wants you to leave. Now!" Becca shouted.

"Ah. So, he doesn't know, does he? I'd suspected as much. Well, don't worry. I'll be happy to tell him. After all, we all know, right?" Kimmie smirked at Cathy, sending a chill to her soul.

Dear God, this is way out of control.

Confusion and a hint of worry creased the corners of Devon's eyes. "What are you talking about?"

Becca tugged on Devon's hands. "Daddy, please. Don't listen to her. Let's go. You and I have a lot to talk about—"

"Daddy? Really darling?" Kimmie leaned in. "We both know he's not your daddy. Actually, all three of us know. Right, Cathy?"

Devon's mouth fell open and she thought he'd swallow the world whole in his grief. Cathy knew in that instant that she'd lost the only man who had ever turned her head and made her feel special. But worse than that, she'd hurt him to the core.

Devon snapped his gaze back to Kimmie. "You're lying."

"For a man who's so suave and worldly, you sure are naïve. Think about it. Why was I in such a hurry to get married? How many months later was Becca born?"

"She was a preemie," Devon insisted.

"At six pound four ounces? Please. You believed what you wanted. You claim that I used you as a trophy, but you weren't any different. You thought you needed a beautiful wife on your arm to succeed, to rise to the top. I turned heads, and you liked that. I knew when I met you that it would be all too easy. You had money and influence and aspirations to go into politics. It was perfect. But you gave it all up when Becca was born. Useless," she muttered with disdain.

"I gave it up to be a proper father and husband. I decided to sacrifice my dreams to be the man you needed me to be. You were fragile and broken. I thought I could heal you."

"You, my dear, were the broken one. You didn't want to realize the truth, but now you have to. Becca isn't your daughter. You have no claim on her."

Devon wavered. The strong, charismatic man that had sauntered into town and Cathy's life was shattering before her.

"Devon." Cathy grabbed his forearm to steady him on his feet. She wanted to comfort him, to heal the wounds his ex-wife had ripped open for the entire town to see.

He snatched his arm away. "Don't."

"I just want to help," Cathy whispered.

Devon shook his head. "You knew, Becca?"

Becca swiped at the tears streaming down her face. "Yes."

"And you?" Devon glared at Cathy then stumbled to the table and grasped the edge, refusing any help from Marcus, Becca, or Rusty.

Cathy swallowed, fighting back tears. "I wanted to—"

"Don't lie to me. I've lived with enough lies." Devon rubbed his temple and lowered into the folding chair in front of him. "How could you?"

Cathy knelt at his feet. "I wanted to tell you. When I found out, I told Becca she needed to tell you immediately. But she needed time."

Becca knelt beside him and placed one hand over his knee. "It's true. I made her promise not to tell you. I wanted to do it myself. That's what I had to talk to you about after the fundraiser. I didn't know how to tell you, but after speaking to Cathy I knew she was right. It was time to face my worst fear, the reason I ran away."

"That's why you left? Because you found out I'm not your father?" Devon's shoulders slumped as if the weight of the truth was crushing him.

"Yes," Becca choked out.

Cathy reached out to him, risking her heart and soul. If he brushed her off this time, she wasn't sure she'd recover, but she had to try to get him to understand. "I know how hard it is to have a child walk out on you. Mine left home and I haven't seen them in years. But your daughter is right here."

"Your kids left because you drove them away,"

Kimmie accused. "I spoke to a few people in town. You're nothing but a busy body, old and pathetic, meddling in everyone else's business because you don't have a life of your own." She folded her arms over her chest. "I still can't believe you're wasting your time on her, Devon. It just goes to show how far you've fallen," she scoffed.

"Stop. You've done enough," Devon roared. A hatred Cathy thought she'd never see on such a gentle face reared up like an angry lion. "You've lied to me all these years. I'm not listening to another word you say. And I'll tell you now, you won't see a dime from me. You should've taken the money when I offered and left, but now, I'll fight with everything I have to send you back to prison and out of our lives."

Kimmie gave a fake gasp. "You have no choice. Go ahead and divorce me, but I'll still get half. I already spoke to an attorney. See you in court." She sauntered from the room, her heels clicking with determination and promise that they hadn't seen the last of her.

"What's going on here?" Judy Benjamin's voice echoed through the rec center.

Cathy spun around to see her standing beside her husband, eyeing the banner above their heads that read *Save baby Amelia*. She closed her eyes, pleading for the world to stop spinning. "It was going to be a surprise," Cathy choked out. "What are you doing back so early? Is Amelia okay?"

Judy nodded. "Actually, she's better than okay. It's not Leukemia. She has a stage 4s neuroblastoma. Apparently at her age, the doctors believe there's a chance the tumor will go away on its own. It's already shrinking."

Sighs of relief spread throughout the room.

"That's amazing news," Cathy said, some of her heartache easing.

"Oh, Cathy. What have you done? I just asked you to watch the shop. For once in your life, I needed you to be a helper, not the center of attention. How could you?"

Devon stood on shaking legs, Becca supporting his elbow. Cathy looked helplessly between her best friend and the man she'd fallen fast for. She'd only wanted to help, to reunite him with his daughter so they could find happiness. To support Judy any way she could. But she'd overstepped her boundaries, turning the people she cared the most about away from her, just like her kids.

Devon glared at her. "Everything I thought about you is a lie. Just like the rest of my life." He jerked from Becca's grasp and stormed from the room, Becca sobbed as she trailed after him.

His words tore through her, shredding every last hope of the happily-ever-after she dreamed of. Her hands shook and her knees threatened to buckle. With that one look, she knew he would forever hate her.

CHAPTER SIXTEEN

Devon finally rolled out of bed mid-morning, packed his clothes and headed outside. He tossed his duffle bag into the trunk of his car then went back inside the inn to settle the bill. Every step took more energy and focus than running a marathon in Florida's summer heat.

All the years he'd chased down his daughter, thinking she'd run away because of something he'd said or done, but she only wanted to get away from him. His heart ached for the time when his little girl would look up at him with soft eyes full of love, instead of the haunted, lost look he now saw.

Had she found her biological father? Was that why he wasn't needed anymore? So many questions plagued him, but he knew better than to ask her. It was time to let her go. He was done chasing her down and forcing her to love him.

He tapped the bell on the front desk and waited for Mrs. Hatfield to totter in from the kitchen.

"Ah, Mr. West. I have a few messages for you from Cathy Mitchell. She also stopped by earlier today. She left this for you." Mrs. Hatfield passed him a large manila envelope.

"Thank you. I'd like to settle my bill, please." Devon slid the envelope from the counter, eyeing the doorway. He wasn't in the mood for Mrs. Hatfield's unique brand of interrogation.

"But it's Christmas Eve. It's time for the town Christmas celebration. You don't want to miss it. There's the Shaw—Mason wedding, too. Should be quite the shindig." Mrs. Hatfield slid on a pair of readers then eyed the old-fashioned wood mail slots behind the counter. "Oh, and there's this, too. A woman who said she was your realtor dropped it off for you."

He nodded in thanks and took the large yellow envelope. No point in telling her he'd changed his mind, but he made a mental note to contact the realtor later.

"Ms. Becca from the coffee shop asked how you were doing. She said she'd stop by tonight after her shift to see you."

He didn't know why she'd want to see him. He was getting out of town, just like she wanted, and she'd never have to see him again. "Thank you," he managed, swallowing the hurt that threatened to consume him. "I'll call her before I head out." Even if he did, he knew she wouldn't answer, but saying otherwise would only invite more conversation from Mrs. Hatfield.

With wallet in hand, he slid out a credit card and slapped it on the counter.

Mrs. Hatfield took the card. "I need to go in the back to run this. Wait here."

Devon leaned against the counter as he waited,

trying to keep himself upright. Several minutes went by, but still she didn't return. His legs threatened to give way, so he sat in one of the chairs near the front door and eyed the envelopes. Finally, he opened the one from the realtor to retrieve the woman's card. No time like the present to call and tell her he'd changed his mind.

The front door opened and Judy Benjamin stepped inside. "Hey, there. I hear you're heading out of town."

Devon nodded. "How did you know? Oh, right. Small town. Mrs. Hatfield probably sent the word out the moment I told her."

"Well, it may seem like we're just a bunch of bored country-bumpkins, but when you live in a small town, everyone kind of becomes your family. We know everyone's business 'cause we love and want to protect each other." She pointed at a chair by his side. "Do you mind if I sit for a minute?"

He didn't feel up to having a heart-to-heart with Cathy's best friend right now, but didn't see any way around it. "Go ahead. I have a feeling my credit card won't be returning without your permission anyway."

"Ah, Cathy was right. You're quick to catch on."

He grimaced at her name.

"I hear you and Cathy hit it off pretty well while I was away."

"That was before," Devon grunted.

"Right. She got involved," Judy chuckled. "You know she just can't help herself. The woman has a big heart, a strong will and can make things happen. It's just that sometimes she lets her desire to help people cloud her judgment."

"Aren't you still mad about the whole fundraiser thing? She must've embarrassed you and your family."

Judy waved a hand through the air dismissively. "Oh, please. Cathy fixed that in a matter of minutes. And everyone in town is pleased the senior center will officially be opening in January. I guess the hearts of the townsfolk were opened when they thought little Amelia wouldn't make it."

"How is she?" Devon wasn't sure why he asked. Even though he was no longer a father, he still empathized with the baby's parents, imagined the anguish they must have felt when they received the news. He also felt a strange connection to the child, one he couldn't quite explain.

"We'll know more in a few hours. My son and his wife are bringing her home. They'll be here in time for the wedding." She shifted to face him more directly. "Listen, I know you're angry. And you have every right to be, but do you believe Cathy had any malicious intent? From what I understand, she only gave your daughter a matter of hours to come clean or she was going to tell you herself. That doesn't sound like a woman that wants to keep a secret."

Devon pulled a piece of lint from his trousers. "No, it's just..." He sighed. Why did he feel so exhausted? "I don't know."

"You thought you'd found a place where you belong, among people who love each other. Trust me. I get it. This town has some sort of pull over people. But ultimately, it's your choice whether you decide to stay.

But I know two women that hope you will."

"Who?"

Judy chuckled. "Cathy was right again. Men can be pretty dense. Your daughter and Cathy, that's who."

Devon shook his head. "Becca isn't my daughter. She's been trying to get me to leave her alone for years, but I never took the hint. Now I know why. I'm leaving so she can have the life she's been searching for all these years."

Judy sighed. "That little girl called in sick for the first time since she moved here. She wanted to find you and tell you how much she loved you. It took her a while, but she finally realized that blood doesn't mean family. You may not be her biological father, but you're the man who raised her, and that's what counts for fatherhood in my book."

"I-I just want her to be happy." Devon shook his head, trying to clear all the conflicting thoughts and emotions swirling inside him.

"Sounds like the best kind of dad to me," Judy said, giving him a smack on the back. "Listen, I hope you stay. Cathy doesn't know I came to speak to you. That woman's way too proud to ask for help from anyone, but I know she feels the same. Becca's actually the one who asked me to speak to you. She doesn't want you to be hurt anymore and she's sorry you found out the way you did. That young woman loves you very much. It broke her heart to leave you, but she'd been under the misguided notion that you knew the truth and had lied to her all those years. Now, she wants to make up for it and be part of your life again, if you'll let her. She and I both hope you'll join us at the town's Christmas Eve party tonight. Everyone and their brother will be there. Trianna Shaw and Jimmy Mason are getting married, too. It's going to be a great place to meet the entire town family."

"I don't belong there," Devon protested.

Judy stood. "Don't you?"

Devon sighed and tossed the paper work from the realtor onto the ottoman in front of him.

Judy froze then bent over to pick up the stack of listings. "Wait. Is this from the realtor?"

"Yes."

Judy shuffled through the pages then stopped at one, studying it for a long moment. "How odd."

Devon leaned over. "What is it?"

"This is Cathy's house." Judy shook her head then handed him the page. Sure enough, the picture showed the same beautiful Victorian he'd spent the night in.

"I knew she was having money problems, but this? I had no idea." She sighed. "Darn stubborn mule." She smoothed out her skirt. "Well, I guess I'll need to have a come-to-Jesus with her tomorrow. I don't know where she thought she was going to live once her house sold, but I'm dragging her hide out to the Benjamin farm to live with us. She won't like it, but I'll just have to threaten her with another horror flick." She chuckled then extended a hand. "It was a pleasure. I hope to see you tonight."

Devon shook her hand, but made no promise to see her later. He was so confused, he wasn't sure where he would be by then.

She headed for the door then paused. "By the way, since Cathy's a proud woman and you dumped her in a rather public way, make sure you're prepared to do a little public groveling if you want her back. And, Devon, you do want her back. God doesn't make women like Cathy Mitchell anymore. She's one of a kind and if you can't see that, you don't deserve her."

The door shut with a thud behind her and he sank back into the seat, dropping his face to his hands. The throbbing pressure in his temple threatened to erupt into a migraine soon if he didn't do something about it.

Everything Judy said about Cathy was true, but she'd still lied to him. He knew it was only at the request of his daughter, but a lie was still a lie.

But did he really have the right to judge her? Wasn't he just as guilty for lying to Becca about her mother being in town? How could he ask his daughter's forgiveness if he wasn't willing to forgive himself?

He lifted the envelope Cathy had left for him and pulled out a rough sheet of white paper. When he turned it over, he gasped. Strokes of color blended together, depicting a scene he'd dreamed of every year since his daughter ran away. Becca sitting by his side next to a Christmas tree. The intricate detail was amazing, as though it had been copied from an actual photo. Every line spoke of the artist's affection for the subjects.

He sighed and looked up at the ceiling, as if God himself would give him advice. "What do I do?"

CHAPTER SEVENTEEN

Cathy admired the large barn-like structure she'd helped design for Sweetwater County. It was *the* spot to have an event, with enough capacity to hold all of Creekside and then some. Tonight it was exceptionally beautiful, with Christmas garlands and twinkling lights intermixed with wedding lace and white roses.

Frank stood on one of the steps, straightening his bow tie. He'd abandoned his usual overalls for a more formal grey jacket paired with old jeans and worn boots. He offered his hand and Cathy smiled. Rusty must have given him a good talking to about his manners.

She clutched his fingers tight. "You look strappin' tonight, Frank."

He smiled, revealing he'd actually taken the time to put his teeth in tonight. "You look prettier than a pair of antlers peekin' over the ridge on openin' day of huntin' season."

Cathy chuckled. Knowing Frank, there was no higher compliment. "How are you still single? A smooth talker like you should've been snatched up already."

Frank straightened. "'Cause I already had my love."

He winked and shuffled away to find some sort of trouble.

She brushed past a group of people she didn't recognize, assuming they were from a few towns over. The annual Creekside Christmas party always drew a big crowd. The entryway glowed with faux candles shrouded in square paper shades. More lights littered the interior, twinkling in wonder. A large Douglas fir filled the room with the aroma of pine that mixed with the apple cider from the beverage table.

"Excuse me." The woman with the scar on her face who'd come into the shop a few days ago stepped forward.

Cathy smiled. "Hi. Grace, right? How are you?"

The woman grinned and guided her child to stand in front of her. "My family wants to thank you for finding the baby Jesus."

The little girl hopped up and down on her toes in excitement. "Yeah. Now we have baby Jesus to watch over us this Christmas. And even Mommy will be home for the holidays."

Cathy shook her head. "But I didn't—"

"Mr. West found it and had it shipped overnight," Grace said. "That's one amazing man you've got. I don't know how he managed it, but it was the best Christmas present ever. Is he here? I'd like to thank him, too. And I still can't believe he wouldn't let me pay him for it."

Cathy fought the tightening in her throat, barely

managing to swallow down the tears. *He'd done all that? But how did he manage with all the commotion?* That man never ceased to surprise her at every turn. "No, I'm afraid not. He's already headed back home."

"I'm sorry to hear that. Are you leaving soon, too?"

Cathy realized Grace assumed they were a couple, but didn't have the heart to correct her. Doing so would only cause the woman unnecessary embarrassment, so she managed a nod and smile instead.

The woman absently touched the scar on the side of her face. "Then please thank him for me."

"Of course, and thank you for coming."

"We wouldn't miss it." Grace glanced around at the surrounding holiday cheer. "It's amazing."

"Mommy, can I get some punch?" The little girl yanked her mother away, making a beeline for the children's sweets table.

Cathy sighed then maneuvered through the crowd, finding a seat in the corner to watch the couples dance. Before yesterday's debacle, she had foolishly hoped Devon would sweep her onto the dance floor. The night would be magical, as would the kiss she'd craved since she'd first spotted him. Christmas had always been a tough time for her, ever since her kids moved away. But this year would prove to be especially difficult.

Why did I send him that drawing? He's probably having a good laugh over it. No, she knew Devon might not like the picture, but he wasn't the type to laugh or judge other people's failures. Yet, knowing that just made her feel worse.

Judy sat down in the chair beside her. "Can I join

you?"

Cathy nodded. "I might call it an early night. Once Trianna and Jimmy get hitched, I think I'll head home. I'm exhausted."

"He still might show." Judy handed her a cup of steaming cider.

Cathy lifted it to her lips and sipped. The rich cloves, mixed with apple, cinnamon, and a little bit of Sweetwater County's special ingredient, warmed her sinuses. "Wow. This year's batch is strong." She coughed and set the cup on the table.

"That's what happens when you're not in charge of everything." Judy nudged her shoulder.

Cathy chuckled. "I don't blame you if you're still mad at me. If there's one thing I've learned recently, it's that I need to butt out of everyone's business. I just make a mess and I'm getting too old to clean up after myself."

"That may be, but without your meddling, things just wouldn't be the same. Nothing would be accomplished around here. I know your heart was in the right place. Besides, everything worked out. I'm just so happy we didn't need your services this time."

Cathy nodded. "So, that neuroblast thing-a-ma-jiggy is going to just disappear?"

Judy straightened her red sweater, her eyes drifting to James across the room. "According to the doctors, the tumor's favorable. In children six months and under, there's a good chance it'll go away. That's what they've concluded anyway, based on the most recent tests. The problem was that the placement of the tumor caused her symptoms to become an issue. Once the tumor started shrinking, Amelia felt much better."

Cathy traced the rim of the plastic cup. "That's great news."

Her gaze rested on the twirling couples in front of her, Cathy saw Trianna and Jimmy enter the Barn. Jimmy scanned the crowd until his gaze settled on Cathy. He waved then Trianna dragged him over to their table.

Trianna bounced between feet. "Cathy, I need you. Everything's falling apart."

Jimmy rubbed his hands down her arms. "It's okay. Don't worry. Everything's going to be perfect."

Judy arched an eyebrow. "As I was saying, this town couldn't function without you. I think you better get back to what you do best. Running things."

Cathy glanced at the garment bag in Trianna's hands. The last thing she wanted to do was help with a wedding after losing Devon, but she couldn't let Trianna down. "Go to the changing room. I'll be there in just a few minutes."

"Thank you." Trianna gave Jimmy a peck on the lips then raced through the crowds of townsfolk and visitors.

Rusty entered with Becca on his arm and clapped Jimmy on the shoulder. "Congrats, man."

"Thanks." Jimmy shook his hand. "I'm one lucky guy."

Rusty's gaze wavered to Becca for a brief moment, then snapped back to Jimmy. "I hope I'm that lucky someday."

Becca joined Cathy at the table. "He hasn't shown?"

Cathy shook her head. "I wouldn't expect him to, darlin'. I'm sure if you give him time, he'll contact you, though. He loves you deeply. He's just wounded right now."

Becca took Cathy's hand in both of hers. "He loves you, too. I've never seen him like that with anyone before. You're special to him. Trust me. I've seen how he behaved around other women in the past. You're the first to ever capture and hold his attention."

Cathy took a long breath, buying time to settle the tilt-a-whirl thoughts swirling in her head. She only managed to squeeze Becca's hand and whisper, "Thank you." Prying herself off her chair, she headed to the dressing room.

Before she could escape the crowds, she spotted Wonda. Based on her derisive grin and fiery eyes, the woman had come to gloat over her failure. *Great. That's the last thing I need,*

"I heard that man of yours left town. Couldn't satisfy him, huh? Maybe next time he'll find a real woman," she sneered as she slipped past.

Cathy clenched her fists. She'd love nothing more than to send the woman rolling down the front steps of the Barn, but she didn't have any time to waste on her, not when Trianna needed her help to get ready for her wedding.

With chin tilted high, she marched to the back of the room and noticed the cupcakes were in the walkway. "Karen, you need to move those to the back table before someone tramples them."

Karen held up two thumbs and began moving the boxes. "By the way, thanks for your help." Her sarcastic tone wasn't lost on Cathy.

"I'm so sorry. Something came up, but you did amazing! They look absolutely delicious." Her diet had already gone to hell from the stress. Besides, a wedding was as good a reason as any to indulge a little.

She entered the dressing room and Trianna clasped her dress to her bosom.

"Oh, good. It's you."

The pale pink material cascaded in waves around her, the white beading catching the light in such a way she looked like a princess. Especially now that she'd gotten rid of that purple stripe in her hair. Although, at a second glance, Cathy spotted the extra two earrings in her left ear. She opened her mouth to protest, but then snapped it shut. It wasn't her place. Trianna was a grown woman and could make her own decisions, no mothering needed. Besides, this was her wedding.

"You look beautiful."

"Thank you, Cathy. Not just for this, but for everything you've done since I came to town." Trianna launched into Cathy's arms.

"Oh dear, you're going to mess up your dress," Cathy protested, but wrapped her arms around the petite girl anyway. "Now, turn around so I can zip you up."

"Right." Trianna twirled around.

When Cathy spotted her barely-there lingerie, she couldn't help herself. "Well, I know Jimmy will be one happy guy tonight." After she managed the zipper, hook and eye, she stepped back. "Let's go get you hitched."

Trianna turned to face her, her cheeks flushed with happiness. Cathy handed Trianna the bouquet she had the florist leave in the dressing room earlier. "When you hear your song, make your entrance, and walk up the main aisle to your husband-to-be."

"Got it. I think I can do that. Well, once my legs start listening to my brain again."

Cathy chuckled. "Don't worry. All brides are nervous on their wedding day." She scooted out the door and nodded to Mrs. Fletcher who sat at the piano to begin the opening music with the soft Christmas carols Trianna had requested. The dance floor cleared and people lined up along either side of a long white runner, congregating near the stage where the ceremony would take place. On cue, Jimmy walked to the front of the room to take his position for the ceremony.

"It all looks beautiful," James said, his arm wrapped around Judy's waist. "You did a great job."

"Thanks," Cathy nodded.

Becca slipped her arm through Cathy's and squeezed. "Promise you'll do mine when the time comes," she whispered. Rusty's face turned beet-red and she feared the poor lad would keel over.

When the first carol ended, Mrs. Fletcher began the second. There would be a total of three before the wedding march. But halfway through the second carol, the song abruptly stopped. Cathy swung around and people parted as if she were Moses. When the dance floor cleared, she spotted Devon standing in the center of the room, an orchid in his hand.

She froze, her heart thumping faster than a hundred wild mustangs racing across an open field. He was dressed in a sage-colored shirt that pulled the traces of green from his dark eyes. She couldn't breathe, talk, nothing that required her brain to function properly.

Becca gasped at her side. "Dad?"

Devon shuffled across the floor and held the Orchid out to her. When Cathy didn't move to take it, he set it on the table next to her then turned to face Becca. "Listen, Becca. I know that a lot has happened and I'm not sure how we'll work through it all, but I'd certainly like to try. I might not be your biological father, but I'll always love you as my own. In my mind and heart, you'll always be my little girl, but I won't pressure you. I understand now that you need to find your biological father and—" His words stopped abruptly as he studied his daughter, tears streaming down her face. "You already found him, didn't you? New York?"

Becca nodded. "I don't know for sure, but I've already decided it doesn't matter. I don't care who my bio-dad is. You're my true father in every way. I'm sorry I've put you through so much."

"Oh, honey. I love you no matter what. You did your best in an impossible situation," he choked out.

Becca launched into his arms and he cupped her head, holding her to his chest.

Cathy fought the tears welling up in her own eyes.

Even if Devon didn't want her after her betrayal, at least she'd brought his daughter back to him.

She went to move around them and restart the wedding, but Devon caught her wrist. He released Becca and kissed her forehead then stepped toward Cathy. Her throat pinched tight as if her body refused to let her speak, fearing she'd say the wrong thing.

"I'm sorry I'm late. I realize I said I'd be here, and it's not gentlemanly to keep a lady waiting." He lifted her hand to his lips, pressing a kiss to her knuckles. Without straightening, he glanced up at her, looking over the top of her hand with that Humphrey Bogart-James Dean effect, just like the first day they'd met. Her body strummed at the music of his voice and the smolder in his eyes.

"Close your mouth," Judy whispered into her ear. "It's not attractive."

Cathy immediately clamped her mouth shut. Every eye in the room was on them, the silence almost deafening.

Still holding her hand in his, he straightened. "Listen, I know I said some awful things. I hope you can forgive me. I guess I believed the worst because that's all I know."

Cathy opened her mouth to reply, but he touched a finger to her lips.

"Don't. I need to say this." Devon took a long accentuated breath. "In you, I see a woman that's everything I've ever dreamed of having in my life. Your compassion and beauty compare to no other. I know now that all you wanted to do was help bring my daughter back to me, yet at the first sign of trouble, I believed the worst." He shook his head. "Even though I knew the information was tainted with lies. I only hope you can forgive me for my rash judgment and give me a second chance. I promise to raise that pedestal and prop you back on top where you belong."

Cathy realized she was holding her breath and exhaled slowly. "I appreciate you telling me. I guess you can leave with a clean conscience now."

"Leave?" His eyes quirked in a funny way. "I'm not going anywhere. I just bought a house." He pulled a folded stack of papers from his coat pocket. "Actually, I put an offer on it, but I hope the lady will accept. I'm planning on renting it back to her until I can move in."

She glanced down at the pages he held out to her and saw the picture of her beloved Victorian. "You want to buy my house?" Her stomach rolled at the inquiring eyes of so many of her friends. She wasn't ready to answer all their questions. "I don't understand."

"I told you I loved your house. And someday I hope to live there with you."

A flash of heat burned her cheeks quicker than a hot flash. "You mean..."

"I mean, I want you to sign a long term lease, hopefully for the rest of our lives. That is, if you'll still have me."

She glanced at Judy, who nudged her in the side. "I'd like you to stay in Sweetwater," she managed, despite the spinning of the room and her emotions.

"Does that mean you forgive me?"

She shook the haze away and straightened. "As

long as you don't put me on that stinkin' pedestal again."

Everyone around them burst into laughter, melting away the tension in the room.

Cathy clasped his hands tight in hers. "In case you haven't noticed, I'm no spring chicken. If I fall off again, I'm liable to break a hip."

"Agreed. Oh, and one more thing. I received your gift and I can't tell you how much it meant to me. You have an amazing talent and I sincerely hope you share it with others. Your drawing had more heart and soul than I've seen in decades."

"I thought I warned you about that over the top flattery, Mister."

"It's not flattery. It's the truth." He rested his forehead on hers. "Honesty. Remember?" At her nod, Devon scooped her into his arms and held her tight. "Now that we're officially courting, there's one more thing I have to do." His lips captured hers with a display that told all of Sweetwater County she was his.

The heat in her cheeks spread to her chest, arms and everywhere else, places she thought had long since died. The faint taste of mint and the smell of his cologne made her feel lightheaded. He tightened his embrace as he deepened the kiss. His tongue tangoing with hers with an expertise she'd expect from a classic Hollywood star. It wasn't until he lessened the kiss that she noticed *it* had happened. Her toes were curled inside her black knee-high boots.

Claps sounded around the room, along with a few hoots.

Devon released her, but kept her close to his side. A smile creased his face with a happiness that matched her own.

"Hey, it looks like we missed all the excitement." Eric Gaylord appeared next to Judy, with Lisa by his side. Judy immediately took baby Amelia into her arms.

Even if Cathy hadn't saved the little girl, the sight of her best friend holding her grandbaby in her arms was prize enough.

"So this is the little one," Devon said, tickling the baby's chin. Amelia smiled, cooing up at him.

Becca offered the baby her finger and Amelia grasped it as though she'd never let it go. "Dad, you sure you're going to be happy in Creekside? I mean, it's not your normal pace."

"Well, I do plan on taking my two favorite ladies to Paris this spring, but otherwise, I have no desire to ever leave Creekside."

The wedding march sounded and gasps drew everyone's attention to Trianna as she entered the main foyer. The crowds instantly cleared the aisle. Standing on the stage, Jimmy's jaw nearly fell off before he managed to collect himself.

As Trianna passed their table, Devon took his daughter in one arm and wrapped his other around Cathy, turning them to face the stage. He whispered to Cathy, "I think your town took hold of me. This *is* where my heart and home belong."

THE END

If you've enjoyed this story please take a second to write a review or tell a friend about what you've read.

For more information please visit
http://www.ciaraknight.com.
Or send her an email at:
ciara@ciaraknight.com

ABOUT THE AUTHOR

Ciara Knight writes to 'Defy the Dark' with her young adult speculative fiction and sweet romance books. Her most recent international best-seller, Pendulum, scored 4 stars from RT Book Reviews, accolades from InD'Tale Magazine and Night Owl Top Pick. Her young adult paranormal series, Battle for Souls, received 5 stars from Paranormal Romance Guild and Night Owl's Top Pick, among other praises.

When not writing, she enjoys reading all types of fiction. Some great literary influences in her life include Edgar Allen Poe, Shakespeare, Francine Rivers and J K Rowling.

Her first love, besides her family, reading, and writing, is travel. She's backpacked through Europe, visited orphanages in China, and landed in a helicopter on a glacier in Alaska.

Ciara is extremely sociable and can be found at Facebook @ciaraknightwrites, Twitter @ciaratknight, Goodreads, Pinterest, and her website ciaraknight.com.

Made in the USA
Charleston, SC
13 October 2016